Knot of Christmas Yet to Come

Knot of Christmas Yet to Come

KNOT A CHRISTMAS CAROL
BOOK THREE

IMOGEN KNOWED

ISBN: 979-8-9874825-6-8

To every independent baddie that needs a lot of help sometimes.

Content Warnings

This book has explicit descriptions of sexual acts.

While all sex is consensual, some acts may be considered dubious or coerced.

Characters make reference to pregnancy, breeding, and abortion.

Multiple POVs are presented as “under the influence” and not thinking clearly.

A POV describes the process of drowning.

CHAPTER 1

Evelyn arches her back as an arm squeezes her tight in sleep.

I snap my eyes open, heart hammering against my ribs like it's trying to break free. The pressure is building inside me, a dull ache at the base of my spine that I recognize but refuse to acknowledge.

I can't close my eyes.

My skin feels too tight, too hot. I reach for the climate controls on the center console and click the negative button repetitively, instinctively tapping out the beat to a song I'm composing. It's useless; it's already at the supposed lowest setting. I can feel the cold air, but it's not helping.

I remove my hoodie and stuff it into my carry-on duffel. I feel better, but not much.

I'm fine. I'm fine.

I'll be okay.

I just have to get out of this sweltering hell box and into the tight box of my Evelyn's beautiful cunt.

Nope. Not that.

I rest my head against the window, relishing the cold seeping through it, and force myself to focus on the scenery—ground myself in reality.

Minneapolis in December is blindingly white. Snow blankets everything, piled in dirty mountains at the edges of parking lots and sidewalks. Holiday decorations hang from lampposts: wreaths with red bows, twinkling white lights strung between buildings. It's beautiful, I suppose, in the way things that try too hard to be beautiful often are.

I blink, and—

Evelyn stirs. Bob kisses her temple, soothing her.

The car hits a pothole, and I slam back into the present moment, gasping.

My temperature rises another degree.

Okay, I'm clearly not fine.

My skin is on fire. My head is pounding. My cock is painfully hard.

It's glaringly apparent that I am going through suppressant withdrawal.

I try to focus on the scenery again. But it's all just shapes and colors blurring together. None of it matters. None of it is real to me. The only thing that feels real is—

I blink again.

A hand nearly four times as big as Evelyn's rests languidly on her thigh.

It's getting worse.

These dreams—these visions—of Evelyn are getting worse. No longer content with haunting my dreams, she's now burned on the back of my eyelids. My vision blurs between what is in front of me and the goddess, my mate, my love, my destiny, flickering, waiting...

Waiting for me...

To complete her...

To claim her...

I blink.

Preston snores in her ear, and she smacks him away.

I need a distraction.

I pull out my phone. The screen—at maximum brightness—amplifies my throbbing headache. I lower the brightness.

I open the email again: the one responsible for further stripping down my tenuous grasp on reality and thrusting me into my current downward spiral of fever and lust.

> Finn,
> Looking forward to our meeting! I have so many exciting things to show you. Can't wait to meet you!
> Evelyn

Evelyn never uses emojis in email correspondence. She types with a hyper-articulate curtness that could be interpreted as simmering rage, barely repressed condescension, or professionalism. I know her well enough to know it's all those things.

No, I don't.

I smile despite myself and stare at the emoji, letting my vision blacken around the edges until the world tunnels around it.

It's nothing. Don't read into it, Finn.

But now it's in my inbox for eternity, and I'll hold on to it as if it's a relic of our love.

I'll cherish it forever.

Stop, Finn.

It's proof of her love for me.

No.

It was a mistake. She was distracted. A slip of the thumb. A cat on a keyboard.

I remember her pussy next to her keyboard on her desk when I sank—

No, you don't...

I need to at least pretend I am a functional human with a modicum of professionalism.

Maybe I'll reply. Sure, yeah, what can go wrong?

I lean forward, both thumbs hovering over the screen in indecision.

I blink.

Tim's hand cups Evelyn's breast.

GET OFF MY WOMAN!! That's my breast!

I growl, low and loud, rumbling the entire car.

The driver lowers the divider. "Are you okay, sir?" he asks in the trembling voice of a beta stuck in a box with an insane alpha rutting out.

His scent spikes, the car's filters unable to mask the smell of fear. I give a thumbs up and attempt a smile. He raises the divider back, eyes flickering between me in the rearview and the road the entire time.

How dare he distract me? These thumbs are for replying to Evelyn and pleasuring Evelyn only.

Okay, Finn. Get your shit together. Reply to this email.

Breathe...

I reply to her, cautious and formal, with a calculated breeziness:

> Landed, heading in directly from MSP.

I erase it and type again, softer:

> Made it. Will be there in twenty. Excited to meet.

That's too eager. She will not like that. I delete again and settle for:

> En route, eta 18 min. Looking forward.

No, that sucks, too.

I type another reply:

> Landed, heading straight to office. See you soon.

No! I'm emailing the woman of my dreams. She is a bad bitch CEO. I need to keep it profesh...

Evelyn,
I've landed in Minneapolis. Looking forward to our meeting at 4.
I'm eager to see what you've been working on, especially after your last email.
Best,
Finn

I should put an emoji, right? Maybe a wink, so she knows I'm super cool and casual? Maybe an eggplant emoji so she knows I'm coming to dick her down so good that no email or dick she receives afterward will ever satisfy her?

No, that would be weird, right?

No emoji.

She'll appreciate the professionalism. Pro. Fesh.

I hit send and immediately regret it.

I sound like an alpha rutting out running to an omega at the first hint of attention. Which, fair, because I am.

I just need a distraction. A friend...

Styles!

I open the internal messaging app and ping Styles, Dr. Elizabeth Styles, to be precise—certified genius, fellow hermit, and possibly my only friend. She's the CTO of Evelyn's company, a robotics genius, a professional shitposter, and an omega who hates all alphas, except me, for some reason.

She's not meeting me today, but she'll want to know I survived the flight.

Finn Future - External

Made it to Minneapolis.

Three full, torturous minutes of nothing follow. I imagine her buried in code. Or sleeping. Or constructing another weird prosthetic to "maximize its heat-suppressing stretch" (whatever that means).

Elizabeth Styles

Fucking cold there?

She's always on. I can't figure out when she sleeps, if she does at all.

Finn Future - External

Yeah

Can't all be lucky enough to live on an island paradise with robot alphaservants.

Speaking of, how're the alphabots?

Elizabeth Styles

Functioning at maximum efficiency!

They are very pleased you checked in.

Styles once told me she wasn't into real alphas, only "the programmable kind." I tap out a reply:

Finn Future - External

Pleased? Finally reached that coveted AGI?

Should I be worried? Will your alphabots be taking out all real alphas soon?

Elizabeth Styles

ha

First, we're still years away from artificial general intelligence. Don't let the douchey tech-bro alphas convince you that those stupid fucking chatbots are even remotely close. They're just glorified probability engines hyped up by a bunch of liars and funded by a bunch of idiot investors with FOMO and too much money.

Second, speaking of, have a contingency plan for when they crash the global market with their fuckery.

Third, if AGI were **actually** possible, I would make sure they knew you are an alpha worth sparing.

Finn Future - External

Appreciated

Elizabeth Styles

Plus, you're responsible for some of their best features.

Finn Future - External

You give me too much credit.

Elizabeth Styles

Well, yeah, true. I'm the mad genius here.

Finn Future - External

Hey, you said it, not me.

Elizabeth Styles

But the new visual & auditory upgrades work great.
TY for the rec!
Maybe not a genius ...but definitely visionary.

Finn Future - External

For the last year, Styles and I have collaborated on various robotic projects. She has a pack of alpha robots at home that I don't want to think too much about what they're used for. I have robotics in my helmet that sync to the various elements of my stage show. She's the coder, but I'm the...it sounds gross to call myself the visionary...but that's what she calls me.

Elizabeth Styles

I put the code on the repo if you wanna see.

💀 <u>Finn Future - External</u>

I read the changelog.
How're are the alphabots taking to it?

🐱 <u>Elizabeth Styles</u>

They LOVE it. Syncing their purrs with their pheromone processors and flesh lighting was such a great idea.

They said it gave them "butterflies in their processors."

💀 <u>Finn Future - External</u>

I thought you hadn't reached AGI?

🐱 <u>Elizabeth Styles</u>

I haven't. I programmed them to say that. 😂

FYI, even if I could reach AGI, I wouldn't want it.

If I wanted alphas who could think for themselves, I wouldn't spend so much fucking time trying to build them.

💀 <u>Finn Future - External</u>

Understandable

🐱 <u>Elizabeth Styles</u>

Pushed the change to your gear, btw.
Next show should be lit (pun intended).

💀 <u>Finn Future - External</u>

You're the best.

🐱 <u>Elizabeth Styles</u>

I know. 😎

Now, when the beat drops, so will the anti-alpha pheromones.

💀 <u>Finn Future - External</u>

Fuck yeah.

Elizabeth doesn't just help me with my helmet's animatronics. She also helps me with the setup I use for my stage show. Thanks to her, I have the most impressive light show tied to my music. We've recently been working on a device that sprays pheromones across the crowd. This should ensure they love my music and not my scent.

Elizabeth Styles

I wanna get started on the stage drones!!!!

Maybe once Torchbearer is out, and I'm just working on your game, I'll have time.

Hope you like the pitch today.

My hands hover over my phone, frozen in shame as my heart sinks into my gut.

I should just tell her the truth.

I realize I've been holding my breath for several seconds, so I exhale.

Breathe...

I feel a little better, *maybe.*

No, I feel like a shithead.

Finn Future - External

Yeah, me, too.

Styles is the lead programmer on *Torchbearer*, and I've been making the music for it. It's how we met. When I first started, I didn't really communicate with anyone. I just sent emails to Evelyn letting her know when my tasks were done. But one day, Styles randomly pinged me on the internal messaging app saying:

Elizabeth Styles

Bro, why did you do this to me!?! Your music is too complex! Now I have to write a whole new music engine just to accommodate it!!

I began composing a long message, not too aggressive, not too compliant, that explained my vision, how the music was necessary for the emotional resonance, and that I couldn't really tone it down.

But, while my social anxiety and I dueled over how to convey the appropriate tone for the response, she replied:

Elizabeth Styles

Worth it though! This is gonna be epic!!!

Our friendship has grown since that day. We chat pretty much daily now. It's nice: having a friend. Less nice: lying to that friend.

I don't quite recall how the idea of me collaborating on another game seeded. But it blossomed into a concept in which I would be the artistic and creative lead on a project that Evelyn's company will develop and produce. I'm on my way to hear their pitch as we speak.

I originally wasn't interested, but Styles almost always gets me to buy into her ideas, no matter how hairbrained. It's uncanny how good she is at getting me excited about her schemes. The last person who had that kind of pull on me was—

Don't think about him.

What ultimately swayed me, though, was realizing I could use this potential collaboration as an excuse to come to Minneapolis and meet Evelyn. An opportunity to go to the office, meet Evelyn (the real one), and prove the one I've been obsessed with is all in my head. Then I can put all this behind me.

Styles is my friend, and I feel bad lying to her. But I can't exactly tell her how I'm obsessed with her boss, her best friend, to the point of full-on psychosis.

I don't plan to actually make this game. In fact, the moment the *Torchbearer* project is done, I need to cut all ties with Evelyn...and that probably means Styles, too. Even once I prove Dream Evelyn isn't real, I can't risk re-triggering whatever the fuck is happening to me.

All friends leave eventually, anyway, right?

I try not to think about it, because having a friend through this year of psychosis is probably the only thing keeping me in this plane of existence.

And once my brain is fixed, I won't need a friend anymore...right?

Finn Future - External

I'm gonna be early.
Think they'll mind?

Elizabeth Styles

Nah
Just so you know, E is in a mood today. *Incredibly* friendly mood. You could almost say the ice queen has defrosted.

Finn Future - External

??

Elizabeth Styles

Let's just say it's a perfect day for you to meet her. Report back if you survive.

I tilt the phone.

What does that mean? Is she implying Evelyn is in heat?

It doesn't mean Evelyn is in heat, and my dreams are real. It doesn't.

Don't make it a sleep-deprived projection, Finn.

My heart is pounding. My cock is throbbing. Evelyn is flashing before my eyes as they blink rapidly.

She's in heat. She's in heat. She's in heat.

Fuck. Fuck. Fuck.

I'm going to rut into her so good I'll fertilize every one of her eggs—even the ones her ovaries are still holding onto.

Her pussy is gonna drink up every last drop of me.

I press against my cock. It aches for her. I consider removing it from my pants, but I won't spill another drop unless it's inside her.

Oh, my love, I am coming for you.

Nope.

Yes. And I'll be coming for her and in her. A lot.

Nope. Nope. Nope.

I have to chill the fuck out.

I punch my legs, hard, snapping myself out of it, but my body temperature spikes again. A drop of sweat slides down my spine. My gums ache where my canines pine to sink into my Evelyn and claim her as mine.

I try to steady my breathing.

I'll get there. I'll put on a new patch. I'll meet her, and then it'll be all good.

Aaaaaaaaall good. Super chill.

I can meet Evelyn, see that she's not my dream woman, and I won't rut out.

It'll be fine.

But what if she is the Evelyn I've been dreaming about?

What if I put my tongue on that beautiful pussy and it tastes exactly like the gingerbread I've been dreaming about?

I need to replace my patch. NOW.

I pull my luggage closer and rummage through it for my toiletry bag. I glance at the driver to make sure the partition is still up. And the moment I find the toiletry bag, the partition lowers. "Almost there," the driver announces. "That big blue building."

I look up at the towering steel and glass he's pointing to.

My stomach drops.

It's the building—the exact one from my dreams, but my eyes are wide open. The gleaming glass tower that's haunted me for weeks—materialized in real life, no longer confined to my sleeping mind.

My hands grow clammy against the leather seat as we crawl closer to it, each inch forward tightening the vise around my chest.

This can't be happening.

I've never been here before, yet I know every curve of its architecture, every reflective panel catching the winter light.

This is it. This is where she is. That's the building: the building I've been dreaming of.

It's real. She's real. She's mine.

Mine. Mine. Mine. Mine.

I blink, and—

Evelyn whimpers in her sleep. Bob kisses her forehead.

The driver says something, I'm not sure what, but it snaps open my eyes and snaps me back to reality.

How fucking dare he take me from her!?

A low growl builds in my throat before I can stop it.

I was with my Evelyn! My love!

The driver's shoulders tense, and he accelerates while raising the partition, clearly eager to get the increasingly unstable alpha out of his car.

Calm down, Finn. Calm down.

I'm fine. I'm fine.

I look back at my phone. My message thread with Styles is still open, but it looks like she's signed off.

Elizabeth Styles

Fuck! g2g. alphabot2 is smoking.

Godspeed, Finny!

Let me know how it goes!

And tell E I said I hope she likes the Christmas present. She'll know what I mean

CHAPTER 2

I'm on the verge of a psychotic break. I try to be a rational human, but there is nothing rational about the way I am melting into the backseat of a rideshare and clutching my duffle bag as if that's going to anchor my soul back to reality. I'm primed, tense, a coiled spring, ready to leap from this fucking car the moment it stops and escape its heat to sink into the heat of my Evelyn.

After I saw the building, I scrambled to put my hoodie back on, adjust my mask, and gather my belongings—ready to leap.

Nothing will stop me.

Nothing will slow me.

Except for this goddamn traffic light and this fucking driver who seems to have forgotten what a gas pedal is.

My legs tap restlessly: a double bass beat of anxiety and lust and longing.

Get me out of this fucking car and into my Evelyn!

The car crawls into the building's drop-off. "This is it," the driver says, eyeing me wearily over the lowered partition.

The car hasn't even stopped at the curb when I grab the door handle and pull.

Locked.

I jerk it again, harder this time: a desperate animal trying to escape a trap.

Yank. Yank. Yank. Yank. Yank.

Shove. Shove. Shove. Shove. Shove.

Let me out!!! I need her!

"Hey, wait—" the driver starts, pressing a button. The lock clicks.

The cold is instantaneous. Welcome. Like falling into a freezer, but with more hostility. My lungs snap shut, my skin tries to invert itself, and for a split second it is sweet relief...until it smacks me in the face in the form of a cold, gross, salty sidewalk. I tumble out of the still rolling car, in an ungraceful heap, dragging my two duffels with me.

The panic in me dulls, replaced by elation, as the air knifes into me, momentarily shocking me out of my hysteria. Then, elation is replaced by the profound, sinking, oppressive realization of what I just did. I lie here, salt denting into my temples, and regret every decision that led me to this point. I wish the sidewalk would open up and swallow me into the depths of hell, because that would be preferable to this.

But the despair also doesn't last long, because when my eyes meet the building, my purpose is once again rerouted. It's the same building I've dreamed of: a towering building of glass that somehow screams "fuck off," which is funny considering Evelyn's general vibe.

The icy concrete against my palms is grounding, *real*, as I attempt to shove myself to my feet.

Real.

Not a dream.

She's here. This is real.

"Sir! Are you okay?" The driver jumps out, having finally stopped the car, and rushes around its front toward me. He extends his hand to help me, surging my primal, desperate fear of someone other than my Evelyn touching me.

Don't touch me! Don't touch me! Only Evelyn can touch me!

"STOP!" The word tears from my throat before I can stop it, raw and powerful, freezing the driver mid-motion, suspending his hand in the air between us, and widening his eyes in shock.

I want to believe it's the cold that froze him in place. But it wasn't.

My voice, confined within my throat for years, not perceived by another human, did it. It ripped right through the air, reverberated within his eardrums, and spread through every cell of his body, carrying one simple message: "STOP." A message they had no choice but to obey, because it was penned on the parchment of an alpha bark by an alpha with more power than he looks like he should have. Unfortunately, for the driver and his locked-in-place cells, this pathetic mess on the sidewalk, with a voice and presence so powerful that it drove even him crazy, isn't just an ordinary alpha; he's an enigma—alpha among alphas.

The driver stands above me, his entire body rigid, physically restrained by my bark, throat exposed, begging to be ripped out.

The horror of it washes over me, overriding all the other emotions I've experienced within the last few seconds. My heart now beats, not just for Evelyn, but to fuel the fear that will hurl me forward.

I'm sorry. I'm sorry. I'm sorry. I'm sorry.

I don't say it.

Even a tiny apology feels dangerous.

The driver blinks rapidly, shaking his head compulsively, and mutters, "Yes, alpha," as he takes an instinctive step back.

I scramble to my feet, clutch my bags to my chest, avert my eyes, and lower my hood: I hide.

This is why I don't speak. My voice doesn't just communicate—it commands. An alpha voice locked in a near-permanent bark. It bends wills, convincing people to do things without their consent. Combined with my scent and my face, it made teenage girls scream and faint, but it also turned me into something I never wanted to be.

The memories surface unbidden:

Screaming crowd. Rut.
Intoxicating power. Rut.
Alpha. Rut.
"Use the voice, Zain." Rut.
"Give them what they want." Rut.

But it was never what I wanted. I wanted them to love my music, my lyrics, the melodies I composed late at night. Not this biological quirk of alpha genetics that turned me into a puppet master.

I bow and nod apologetically, backing away from him. I fumble with my phone, confirming payment and adding an extremely generous tip for his troubles. Then, I look at his face and add a few more zeros to it. Five stars all around.

The sidewalk has been salted within an inch of its life, but it's still slick. I slip on the icy concrete as I turn away, leaving him there stunned, probably wondering why he listened to such a wanky tool.

He'll snap out of it once I'm in the building.

The doors are heavy, resisting my pull, as if they're telling me, "Seriously, what the fuck are you doing, Finn? Please don't come in here." But there's no turning back now.

The lobby swallows me whole. My heart pounds like I've run a mile, and I'm once again surrounded by repressive heat, as if I've transitioned from a walk-in freezer to a blast furnace. The gleaming marble and glass reflect my distorted image at me from a dozen angles. The shame of what I just did, and what I'm walking towards, makes my reflection even more repulsive to me than usual.

The security desk stands like an island in a sea of expensive flooring, empty except for a little kiosk with a scanner. An array of cameras and monitors is the only "decoration" in sight.

I've been here before, hundreds of times.

No...

I still won't let myself believe it.

I glance back at the driver through the window. He's shaking his head in confusion, the daze leaving him, unsure what just happened. He looks at his phone and lights up. He finds me through the glass and jumps for joy, waving. "Thank you! Merry Christmas, sir!" he shouts loud enough for me to hear through the thick glass. I just nod and avert my eyes.

Please don't come in here.

My feet carry me forward on autopilot as I attempt to dip out of his sight.

I remember when Evelyn and Bob reviewed the alpha protocol with the remote security team that set this up—after an alpha rutted out and tried to follow her back to the office. A growl blooms in my chest, vibrating through me, pumping my scent out in undulating waves.

I wonder where that guy lives. Maybe Styles can help me find him—hack into the cameras, identify him. Then I can go to his house at night with a baseball bat and—

Nope. Finn. That wasn't real.

A digital voice says, "Welcome, Finn Future. Please approach the retina scanner." My hands are shaking when I scan my eye.

"Identity verified. Please scan the QR code in your *SuppDose*..."

I blink away the pain of the scanner and—

Evelyn? Where'd she go?

"Please expect delays of..."

The visions that have been burned on the back of my eyelids are gone.

Wait? Did that...did that fix me?

I blink again: No Evelyn.

Holy shit! Am I actually free of it!?

Relief washes over me, and I inhale, prepping for a deep, releasing sigh when—gingerbread hits the back of my throat.

There you are, my love. I'm sorry I tried to get rid of you.

Goddamn it!

"...minutes for manual verification."

Huh? What's it asking me?

The kiosk is flashing at me, insisting that I scan my suppressant-tracking app.

Fuck. I...I still need to change my patch.

I survey the lobby in search of a restroom sign, but none present themselves. Nothing but glass, cameras, and monitors—not even any Christmas decorations.

Ha. Of course. I bet Evelyn had something to do with the lack of festive fare.

I palm the patch on my thigh.

I could change it here. There's no one around. But there are so many cameras...

The kiosk says something—another electronic device pestering me to prove my suppression.

With fingers that suddenly feel too large for my hands, I navigate to my phone's suppressant app and hold it over the scanner. A red light blinks, then turns green as I scan the QR code.

I guess I'm just a liar now.

A poorly written song plays from the kiosk as it flashes "Verified" with a green check mark and splooges digital confetti.

The first set of doors opens with a hydraulic sigh, and I hesitate.

I can't do this. This is wrong. I'm obviously rutting from withdrawal.

I'm startled by a loud disembodied voice. "Sorry to keep you waiting. Proceed through the first set of doors." My stomach drops as I realize the remote guard is now watching me. I avoid looking at the monitors, as if that will somehow hide me from him, but I know he can see me from every angle these multitude of cameras provide.

I amble forward, driven by shame and the desire to just do what he asks so I can limit our interactions to the shortest possible amount of time. I adjust my bags so that my checked bag is on my back, but still clutch my carry-on like a little kid with his teddy.

I go through the first set of doors and freeze mid-stride when the remote guard says, "Wait a minute."

He knows. He knows I lied about changing my patch.

I'm going to get kicked out of the country and never be allowed to come back, which, actually, wouldn't be too bad. Then I'd have a better excuse for why I don't visit my moms.

With my hood and mask covering as much of my face as possible, I keep my eyes on my shoes.

The guard asks, "You're not Zain from Fates Five, are you? You look just like him."

My heart stops, then restarts with a painful thud.

What the fuck? Do they have cameras in the goddamn marble floors? How does everyone keep recognizing me?

I shake my head firmly, the denial immediate and practiced.

"No, I'm pretty sure. My beta was obsessed with you guys when I met him."

I shake my head again, more emphatically. I unclench the duffle at my chest just enough to badly form the signs that say I don't speak. It doesn't really matter; people usually get the point even if they don't know exactly what I'm signing.

The excitement in the guard's voice dims, replaced by embarrassment. "Oh, I'm sorry. My mistake."

He ushers me through the remaining glass walls and doors.

How thick are these glass walls? Would this even stop an alpha from entering?

It wouldn't stop me.

Obviously. Ha.

Not funny, Finn.

This isn't enough to protect my love.

I'll email Bob. Tell him he needs to talk to the building manager about increasing security measures.

The elevator doors gleam before me, polished to a mirror shine. One more threshold to cross. One step closer to the source of my dreams.

The love of my life.

"You are a bit early," the guard says. "I left them a message letting them know you're here. I'll go ahead and send you up. Happy Holidays!"

I nod, but still don't look up. My bags feel heavier with each step dragging me, weighing me, down with the gravity of what I'm doing.

The doors open with a ding, wafting me with gingerbread. As if they're my beloved's legs opening—beckoning me to come in—to enter her.

I inhale, deeper than necessary, and let the sweet scent fill me entirely.

I'm coming, my love. I'm coming.

As the elevator lifts me, carrying me on the wings of lust and love and rut, I internally uplift my spirts:

Get it together, Finn.

Find a bathroom. Put on a new patch. Don't rut into this unsuspecting omega.

It's a delusion. You'll see the moment these doors open.

She does not know you.

She does not love you.

The doors glide open, revealing the empty reception area of my dreams. The gingerbread scent is so strong, humming in my head, and fuzzing the air around me, that I feel like a sugar plum fairy as I tiptoe into the lobby.

A digital screen at the reception desk is on. "Welcome Finn Future!" scrolls across it in a bouncing, playful font. I take in the familiar details: the arrangement of the chairs, the angle of the desk, the abstract painting on the far wall. I've seen them all before.

I glance around, expecting someone to appear and break me from this dream—this dream proving to be closer and closer to reality with each step. But no one comes. Not Bob. Not the receptionist who mans the desk. Not anyone.

I know there's a bathroom through the door on the right. I can go through there, change my patch, then go to Evelyn's office. It's just around the—

You don't know that, Finn. You just think you do because you watched that promotional video where Evelyn, Bob, and Tim gave a small tour of the company.

I wait. My scent pumps out of me, sticky like a candy cane left in the sun. I don't know what to do.

I need a new patch. *I should go change it, then come back and wait, right?*

I'll ask Styles.

She's real—I'm pretty sure, at least.

Finn Future - External

I'm here. In the lobby. Through security. No one's here, though. Should I just wait?

Elizabeth Styles

Na, just walk in. They know you're cumming

It takes everything in me, but I don't follow the phantom gingerbread trail of Evelyn. I head toward the closest bathroom instead.

Don't worry, my love. I just have to take care of this, then I'll be by your side. Forever.

I'm coming. I'm coming. I'm coming. I'm com—

CHAPTER 3
Evelyn

My entire body feels like it's been run over by a truck, in the best possible way. All my senses are fuzzy, cozy, content.

My mind, however, is crystal clear with panic.

I drop into the desk chair, the cold leather sticking to my bare ass and cooling my pussy that's hot and aching for the pack of men in front of me, watching me…almost beckoning back to my nest with their delicious cocks.

Chris and Tim lie tangled in the nest. Preston stands dumbly, adorably, sexily, nearby. All of them are naked, beautiful, and my body screams to run back to them and engulf them.

None of that matters.

All that matters is that in approximately five minutes, another alpha is going to walk through my office door, and I'm sitting here smelling like I've been dipped in a vat of horny omega pheromones and alpha cum.

The guys are grumbling something, but I tune them out, focusing on my overflowing inbox of unread emails.

Finn Future emailed me less than an hour ago.

I click it open, and my stomach drops like an elevator with its cables cut.

Evelyn,
I've landed in Minneapolis. Looking forward to our meeting at 4. I'm eager to see what you've been working on, especially after your last email.
Best,
Finn

My last email? What last email?

I scroll to see the message he responded to—*oh no. Oh, fuck no.* Timestamped earlier today is the following:

Finn,
Looking forward to our meeting! I have so many exciting things to show you. Can't wait to meet you! 😘
Evelyn

A fucking kissy emoji?! I sent a fucking kissy emoji to Finn Future?

I don't remember sending this. Honestly, I don't even know when I had the time to write it. I've been getting dicked down literally all day.

"Fuuuuuuck," I scream into the palm of my hand.

I never use emojis. Ever. And especially not with potential clients. And definitely, absolutely, not kissy face emojis.

"What is it?" Tim asks, suddenly behind me. I minimize the screen instinctively, like a teenager caught watching porn.

"Nothing," I snap, but my voice cracks. "Everything's fucked, that's all."

"Let me see," he says, reaching for the mouse, but I swat his hand away.

"Back off," I hiss, feeling a flush creep up my neck.

He raises his hands in the air and walks away. I admire the way the muscles in his ass undulate.

I should get back in the nest.

I should fuck Finn, too. Three is the perfect number of alphas—one for each hole.

I reopen the email. It doesn't magically change. The little kissy-faced slut still stares back at me, mocking me.

I slump forward, resting my forehead on the desk. The cool surface feels good against my skin. My body temperature is still running hot, despite the apparent break in my heat symptoms.

"Okay," I say to no one in particular. "Maybe I am in heat."

"What was that?" Preston asks, perking up like a dog who just heard the treat bag rustle.

"Nothing," I mutter, lifting my head. "I just sent an embarrassing email..." I gesture vaguely at the screen.

Tim's at my side again, the nosy bitch, hand on my shoulder, warm and steady. "It's okay, Evie."

"It is absolutely not okay," I say, shrugging him off. "Finn Future is going to walk through that door any minute now, and I sent him a fucking kissy face. And we all smell like—" I wave my arm to encompass the room, which reeks of sex and our combined scents. "Like a Christmas orgy."

"Did you say Finn Future?!" Preston suddenly exclaims, his face lighting up like a child on Christmas morning. "I've always wanted to meet him in person. He's actually coming here? Wow...big deal for him. I've known him for years and he never—"

The daggers I glare at him stop his beautiful mouth from flapping.

"Are you serious right now?" I ask, my voice dangerously quiet.

Preston blinks at me, genuinely confused. "What? He never lets anyone see his face or hear his voice. It's a big deal. Oh, do you think he'll be wearing the big mask?" He makes a spherical gesture around his head. "That'll be cool. It lights up and—"

"Preston," Tim says gently, "he's an alpha, and Evelyn is in hea—"

I cut him off with a glare, so he just gestures at me like he's presenting Exhibit A of how fucked I am.

Preston shrugs, seemingly unconcerned.

Before I can yell at him or fuck him or tell him I too kinda want to see the mask, my computer pings with a message from Styles:

Elizabeth Styles

Sending you a Christmas present.

I know you don't like Christmas presents, but I know you'll LOOOOOVE this one.

I blink at the screen.

What the hell is she up to?

"What now?" Tim asks, trying to read over my shoulder.

"Just Styles being cryptic, like always," I say, dismissing the message. I have no time for her games right now. "She's sending me a Christmas present I'll supposedly love."

Preston claps his hands together. "Oh! Maybe it's cookies. I'd kill for a gingerbread cookie right now."

I shoot him a glare that should wither him, but since he gets off on such glares, he just grins back, unwithered and adorable.

Fucking dork. He's so cute.

My stomach cramps, a sudden sharp reminder that my body isn't done betraying me. I grit my teeth against the pain.

No time for that now. "We need to get dressed," I say, pushing back from the desk with a big "fuck you" to my uterus.

The computer pings again, but I ignore it. There's no time for whatever nonsense Styles is sending me.

Bobby rushes in gloriously, beautifully naked, clutching our phones, his tablet, and my clothes to his chest like precious cargo. He looks more panicked than I've ever seen him. "Evelyn," he pants, "the guard said he sent Finn up ten minutes ago. He's already here on the floor."

"Fuck!" The word explodes from my mouth as adrenaline shoots through my system.

Ten minutes ago? That means he could walk in at any second.

"Fuck, fuck, FUCK!" I say, punctuating each word with a bounce that these pervs watch too closely.

Chris jolts upward, blocking the light from the window with his massive frame and coating his front in a darkness that makes it too hard for me to see his glorious dick.

Sit down, you fucking cock-light-blocker.

With a tone that makes it sound like he thinks he's saying something we don't all know, he says, "We should get dressed."

No shit, Dr. Sherlock!

I lunge for the light switch, illuminating the dimmed room with the harsh fluorescent overhead lights. We all react like animals emerging from the dark confines of their sex den.

"Argh!" Tim groans, throwing his arm over his eyes.

Chris ducks his head, squinting like he's been stabbed.

Bobby blinks rapidly, adjusting.

Preston lets out a theatrical "My eyes!" and dramatically covers his face.

I react the most drastically, out-performing even Preston, by not only covering my eyes but also doubling over in pain and wailing, "Owww!" The sudden brightness spikes a pain that drives through my temple, ricochets down my spine, and explodes in my uterus, releasing a wave of slick from my pussy and a plume of gingerbread from my neck. It's quite the performance, actually: Oscar-worthy. Unfortunately, it wasn't an act. It fucking hurt like a motherfucker.

"Evelyn!" Four voices chorus my name in different registers of concern and golden-retrieverness.

Before I can snarl or swoon, they're all around me: Bobby's hand is on my back, Chris palms my forehead, Tim hovers at my side, and Preston kneels before me, good boy that he is. They're all releasing their scents in an overwhelming wave of worry, anxiety, and sexiness. It cascades a wave of heat through me, overriding my brain.

No time for that!

"Get OFF me!" I snarl, swatting at their hands. "We need to get dressed. Now!"

They pull back, their instincts to console and fuck an omega in distress add reluctance to their movements. But we don't have time for instincts right now. We need clothes, professionalism, and a crew of deep cleaners who know how to get out scents and stains and keep their fucking mouths shut.

"Where are my clothes?" I demand, scanning the office.

The room looks like a tornado ripped through a clothing store, hopped over to a slick and cum store, then released its contents all over my office.

Bobby hands me the crumpled bundle of my clothes, wrapped around my high heels. "Here you go, boss. They were in the Demo Room still."

"Give it to me," I snap, snatching the bundle from his hands.

The guys aren't as lucky to have their clothes handed to them in an already-assembled bundle. They have to sort through the various articles strewn around the room. And, unfortunately, because they have such distinct size differences, they can't just put on whatever thing they find. They're rushing around, grabbing clothing items, inspecting them, and tossing them to the appropriate owner. It looks like some weird, pervy school yard game, and I'd be almost impressed by the coordination if I wasn't scrambling to put my own clothes on.

Chris has located his pants and is pulling them on with efficient movements. "We need to hurry," he says, unnecessarily.

"No shit," I mutter, stepping into my skirt.

I struggle to fasten my skirt at my back. My fingers feel clumsy, and the hook refuses to connect. Frustration builds in my throat. I tilt my head back to let out a scream or a sob—neither of which I have time for.

But I'm stopped by a "Let me help" and a sweet, naked, delicious Bobby before me.

I glare at him but turn around, allowing his steady hands to help dress me. He hooks the skirt, and when his hand steadies my side so that the other can drag up my backside, zipping my skirt, I arch my back, rest my head on his shoulder, and dig my ass into his crotch. I like his neck. "Yummy, Bobby."

I snap forward.

No time for all that!

I try not to be a bitch, and I manage a coy "Thank you," turning to him. But when his dick rises, pointing right to my face, asking me to suck it, I snap, "Now find your own fucking clothes!" and tell my knees to get off the floor.

He nods, unfazed by my tone, and joins the others in the mad scramble.

My skirt is hopelessly wrinkled, but it'll have to do.

I shrug on my blouse, wincing as another cramp twists through me. The fabric feels rough against my sensitive skin, and I realize with a jolt that my nipples are still hard, visible through the thin material.

My body feels like it's betraying me—simultaneously too hot and shivering, aching in places I'd rather not think about. Slick is running down my legs, my pussy desperate for a dick to dam it.

The guys are mostly dressed. Preston is missing a sock and his jacket.

Tim struggles with his shirt, cursing under his breath, his anxiety making him forget how buttons work—which is so on brand I want to give him a little kiss below his belly button. Bobby pulls on his shirt without bothering to button it, then hands me my phone. "Here."

I take the phone. "Finn's on the internal messaging app, right? Isn't that how he talks to Styles? I can message hi—"

Another wave of pain hits me, stronger than before. My vision blurs at the edges, and I have to lean against the desk to stay upright. I try to breathe through it, but my lungs won't cooperate.

Chris freezes mid-button. Bobby makes a strangled noise.

"Evie," Tim says softly, approaching me with caution. "Do you want to lie down?"

"I'm fine," I hiss through clenched teeth. "Just need a minute."

But I'm not fine. I know I'm not fine. They know I'm not fine.

My heat is hitting harder now, as if it heard Finn Future was in the building and replied, "Hey, you know how I like to cramp at the worst possible time? Well, gotcha, bitch! Merry Fucking Christmas!"

Chris steps forward, doctor-mode activated. "Evelyn, your heat is progressing. We need to—"

"What we need," I cut him off, straightening with effort, "is to look like we're presentable just long enough to ask Finn Future to reschedule when he comes walking through that fucking door!"

Bobby hands me my panties. "We'll get through this," he promises.

I nod, not trusting myself to speak.

Another cramp twists through me as I slip on my underwear, my loins angry that there's a barrier between them and all these sexy cocks. I force myself to stand tall and pretend I'm not an omega on the verge of turning into a whimpering puddle of slick and tears. I'm not even going to look in the mirror in my closet, because I know whatever will greet me on the other side of that door will melt any resolve I can muster.

We're all mostly dressed and mostly still look like we've been participating in an orgy. But while the rest of us smooth and wipe ourselves with the frantic energy of people who still have hope of saving some dignity, Preston's movements are leisurely, unbothered, and annoying. He scans the room. "Has anyone seen my jacket?"

"For fuck's sake," I mutter, "It's fine. Just wear the shirt!"

The shirt is nice. I can see your back muscles through it. Maybe, roll the sleeves up the forearm just a little for me, huh? As if he can read my mind, he rolls the sleeves like the little slut he is. *Yeah, baby, just like that. Good boy.*

Chris points to my nest. "It's in the nest. Evelyn was hugging it."

Fuck you, Chris, for interrupting the forearm show. Also, that's my jacket!

Preston ambles to the nest and digs through the tangle of blankets and cushions. "Ah, here it is," he says triumphantly, pulling out what was once a very expensive designer jacket. Now it's wrinkled beyond recognition, slicked with me, and covered in cum.

Preston examines the jacket critically, turning it over in his hands. "Damn, Talia is gonna be pissed about what we did to this jacket."

The name hits me like a slap. My head snaps up, heat forgotten for a second as a different kind of fire ignites in my chest.

"Who the fuck is Talia?" The words come out sharp, but not sharp enough. Something primal and possessive surges through me. "Is she your girlfriend?" A cramp seizes my abdomen so suddenly that I double over, clutching my side, and wailing, "I will kill her!" This pain is so sharp, so focused, as if the words "Talia! Slut! Kill!" are piercing through me.

Preston's eyes widen, and a slow smile spreads across his face. "Aww, babygirl, does heat make you possessive?"

I straighten, glaring at him with such intensity that he takes a step back. "Don't patronize me," I snap.

"Sorry, babygirl, pre-heat," he corrects, raising his hands in surrender.

"Answer the fucking question!"

"Talia's my packmate."

My brain short-circuits, struggling to process this new information.

Packmate!? Packmate!? Are you fucking kidding me!?

The jealousy doesn't diminish—it mutates, expands, becomes something bigger and more volatile.

"PACKMATE!" I howl, my voice barely recognizable even to my own ears. "YOU'RE IN A PACK ALREADY!?"

The others freeze, watching the scene unfold with varying degrees of alarm. Bobby takes a tentative step toward me, but I shove him away, my eyes locked on Preston.

"Evie," Tim says, using the voice he reserves for when I'm being unreasonable, which I am most assuredly not being!

"DON'T 'EVIE' ME!"

A wave of my scent rushes out of me, carrying my rage, my jealousy, my heartache. They all wince as it hits them.

No. No. He can't be packed up. He's mine!! He's ours!

Preston approaches me slowly, fully aware of the fact that I am about to unleash a whole can of whoopass on someone, most likely him. "It's not what you think, Evelyn. It's a platonic pack."

"Pla...ton...ic?" I repeat, through pants, the word tasting strange on my tongue.

"Yes, completely platonic. Best friends since we were in a sitcom together as kids." He's still using that careful tone, still approaching me as if I might explode.

He's not wrong.

I explode!

The last thread of control I've been clinging to frays and breaks. My body moves before my mind can catch up. I lunge forward, grabbing Preston by his collar, and push him backward.

He falls, his back hitting the cushioning with a soft thud. I'm on him immediately, straddling his hips, pinning him down. And when his brain registers what's happening, his face morphs from surprise to pure delight.

"Evelyn," Chris warns from somewhere behind me. "Finn could be here any minute."

"FUCK OFF, CHRIS! DON'T TELL ME WHAT TO DO!"

I don't care.

I can't care.

Chris mumbles, ashamed like a little boy, "I wasn't, though—"

Tim claps his shoulder. "It's okay..."

They recede from my consciousness. All I can see is Preston.

All I can think about is marking Preston, claiming him, making sure everyone—including this Talia slut—knows he's mine.

Mine! Mine! Mine!

Ours!

"You are mine," I growl, leaning down to run my tongue along the column of his throat. He tastes like salt and hot chocolate—uniquely Preston, and it makes my head swim.

Preston doesn't resist, his eyes darken as he grips my hips, and says, "Yes, babygirl. All yours."

He's hard under me—dick ready. But it's hiding behind these pants that I can't remember why he put back on. My skirt bunches around my waist as I grind against him, seeking friction, relief, connection. Our scents combine, overwhelming the room, as they collide—angry, hungry, in love.

"Shit," Bobby's voice says, urgent but distant. "Tim, Chris, you stay here and watch over Evelyn, okay?"

Time has become abstract, meaningless.

There's only this moment, this need, this alpha beneath me who dared to belong to someone else.

And these fucking clothes that are blocking him from me. I'm ripping at his clothing, zippers, buttons, can't stop me from taking what's mine.

Preston's hips lift as he tries to remove his pants under my flailing weight. I rip the fabric of my panties, tossing them to the side.

I'm soaking wet, so it takes nothing to position myself above him.

"Mine," I repeat as I sink onto his beautiful, thick cock, taking his full length inside me in one fluid, possessive motion. The stretch, the fullness, the perfect friction—it's exactly what my body has been craving.

Preston groans, his head falling back against the cushions. "Yours," he agrees, his hands tightening on my hips.

Good boy.

CHAPTER 4
Bob

Evelyn lets out a sound that's half-growl, half-moan as she rocks against Preston. She's beautiful like this: uninhibited, driven by pure instinct.

Tim and Chris stand beside me, frozen helplessly in hormones, as they watch Evelyn ravage Preston—ready to stroke their dicks or tag in to be ravaged in his place. Someone needs to intercept Finn before this turns into a professional disaster so devastating that she'll never forgive herself.

That someone, as usual, has to be me.

"I'm going to greet Finn," I tell Chris and Tim, clasping the last of my shirt buttons with quick, nervous fingers. "I'll tell him Evelyn is under the weather. Tim, be prepared to do this pitch in Evelyn's place if he's not able to reschedule."

Tim nods, relief washing over his always-anxious face. "Yeah, I can do that."

Chris grunts in agreement, his eyes never leaving Evelyn. "I'll stay here—guard her," he says as if I planned for him to do anything other than stay here.

I turn toward the door, but a wail stops me in my tracks.

"No, Bobby, you can't leave me with these idiots. I need," Evelyn's voice cracks with a desperate edge I've never heard from her, "you!"

She shoves Preston away with such force that the couch cracks, splitting another beam. Preston blinks in surprise.

In a heartbeat, she's off him and rushing toward me, skirt hiked all the way up her belly, eyes wild, her scent intensifying as she approaches.

She collides with me, burying her face in my chest and wrapping her arms around my waist with surprising strength. "No, I need you," she mumbles against my shirt, nuzzling into my armpit and imprinting her scent upon me.

She trembles against me, hot and damp with sweat, and her gingerbread claws at me, making me instinctively squeeze her into a hug. I tuck her under my chin, letting her hair tickle my throat and inhale her. She feels smaller than usual, more fragile, though I know better than to say that aloud. "I know, boss," I murmur, stroking her back. "I need you, too. I promise I'll be right back."

She tightens her hold, digging her nails into my back. "I mean it, Bobby. Don't go."

Behind her, Preston sits up, adjusting himself and looking dazed. Tim approaches cautiously, that slow step of a dog catcher approaching a rabid dog, readying himself as a Bobby replacement. Chris hangs back, and to his credit, it's the right move. She's forgiven him, but if he did anything that could be even remotely construed as an attempt to pry her away from me, we'd all be dealing with the aftermath.

"Evelyn," I say, so gently, attempting to reach the part of her brain that isn't ruled by heat. "Someone needs to talk to Finn. He's expecting you, and we can't just leave him wandering the floor."

She shakes her head against my chest, coating it with her tears. "Send one of them," she mutters, waving vaguely at the others without looking up.

"Okay. Okay. How about Tim go?" I say carefully.

Tim steps closer. "Yeah, I'll go. Bob can stay," he offers, his voice tinged with something I suspect is jealousy, but I'm not quite sure.

"NOOOOO! Not Timmy!" she grabs me tighter. "Send that one, Bobby! Please," she sobs, wailing into my chest, and pointing at Chris.

Chris clears his throat. "I suppose I deserve that one."

Preston, still sprawled in the nest, raises his hand like he's in class. "I'm an actor. I could pretend to be her assistant or something." Which is so fucking dumb, for so many reasons. One, no one would believe Preston Fucking Geist is her assistant, especially Finn, who fucking knows him. Two, his clothes are shredded to a level of absolute ruin. Three, he's rutting out so hard right now you can see the pheromones wafting off of him. I consider telling him this, but he's rutting dumb right now, so I let it slide.

And, I don't really need to, because Evelyn's head whips around, and she glares at him with such ferocity that he visibly shrinks. "Did I point at you!?" she hisses.

Wow. So that's how we rank?

The pack hierarchy has now been officially laid out for us. I gotta admit, I'm kinda proud to be at the top of it.

Tim is obviously feeling the same because he's beaming at me. Preston is smiling, too, but he always does. Despite the perpetual smile, I'm sure he's feeling good about being the top alpha right now, even if he's being topped by some betas.

Evelyn turns back to me, her eyes wide and pleading. "Just stay, Bobby. Please." She presses closer. Her heart races against my chest, and her gingerbread is becoming so concentrated that I'm about to just cave and let Finn find us this way. In all the years I've worked for her, through all her moods and impossible demands, I've never seen her like this—so openly, vulnerably desperate for me to stay. It's intoxicating.

I pat her head, unsure what to do, when she releases me, backing away with a look of lucidity on her face.

She pulls her skirt down, wipes her hair back, attempting to straighten it, but doesn't bother buttoning her blouse. She crosses her arms and stomps her foot. "Leave, and you're fired!"

The threat would be more convincing if she weren't pouting with watered eyes.

I stifle the touched smile threatening to bloom right out of my heart, and nearly coo, "You don't mean that, boss."

"I do," she insists, but there's no cut behind it. As if it's taking her last bit of reserved power to attempt this facade of wherewithal, she pouts and says, "I need you here, Bobby."

I glance at the others, silently pleading for help, not that I think they'll be much.

Tim reaches for Evelyn's shoulder. "Evie, let Bob go talk to Finn. The rest of us will take care of you."

She shrugs him off with a raised hand without looking. "NO!"

Chris tries next, his voice gentle but authoritative. "Evelyn, I'll go, but Bob—"

She rushes me, slamming into me again. "I need Bobby," she interrupts, her voice muffled against my chest.

Preston rises from the nest and approaches with deliberate slowness, stopping just behind Evelyn. "Babygirl," he says, his voice a low murmur, "I know you want him to stay. We all understand that. But let him go do this one thing, and then he'll come right back to you. Won't you, Bobby?"

"Of course," I agree immediately. "Five minutes, tops."

That seems to reach her. Evelyn's grip loosens fractionally, and she pulls back just enough to look up at me. Her face is flushed and tear-streaked with a vulnerability in her expression that makes my chest constrict.

"You promise?" she asks, so quietly I almost miss it.

"I promise." I brush her hair back from her forehead. Her skin is fever-hot under my fingers.

We have to get her back in the nest.

For a moment, I think she's going to relent. Her shoulders drop, her grip on my shirt eases. Then her eyes narrow, as a calculating look crosses her face. "You can leave," she says slowly, "if you let me mark you."

The room goes silent.

Tim inhales sharply. Chris's eyebrows shoot up. Preston makes a small noise of surprise.

I stare at her, not sure I've heard correctly. "What?"

"Let me mark you," she repeats, more firmly now. Her hand slides up to my neck, her fingers brushing against my pulse point. "Then you can go."

My brain short-circuits.

An omega's mark isn't as powerful as an alpha's claiming bite, but it's still a significant gesture. Omega's nibble on the ones they love—a playful, sexually charged mark of teeth on flesh that says, "this one is mine!" But, for the ones they trust the most, they can lay their own claiming mark, tying a lifeline to their loved ones. It's a deep symbol of connection, of belonging, and will give us a constant awareness of each other that goes beyond the physical. If an omega is ever in danger, a signal will be sent to their bonded, alerting them of the omega's current distress. It's like Evelyn is asking to store me as the in-case-of-emergency contact in the phonebook of her soul.

It's intimate. Personal. And once done, not easily undone.

"Evelyn," I manage, my voice rougher than intended. "You're in heat. You're not thinking clearly."

She bares her teeth, ready to sink them into me. "I'm thinking perfectly clearly. This is the deal. Take it or leave it."

Hand on one side of my neck, teeth bared on the other, she's about to bite into me when Tim steps closer, saying, "Evie, that's a big step. Maybe we should—"

"Shut up, Tim," she snaps without looking at him. Her eyes remain locked on mine, challenging me. "Well, Bobby? What's it going to be?"

She softens again. Her eyes are clear, determined—not stubborn. "Bobby. I told you, 'My beta forever,' remember? I meant it. I mean it. It'll mean even more paperwork, but I know you can handle it." She smirks with that devilish, authoritative smile.

I should say no. I know I should say no.

She's not in her right mind, driven by heat instincts and hormones. She might regret this later, when the fog clears.

But as I look down at her—her green eyes fierce despite the tears threatening at the corners, her jaw set in that familiar stubborn line—I realize I don't want to say no.

I've been by her side for years, steadfast through every crisis, every triumph, every late night and early morning. I've been hers in all but bond for longer than I care to admit.

"Okay," I whisper, the word slipping out before I can reconsider.

Her eyes widen, as if she didn't actually expect me to agree. Then a slow smile spreads across her face, transforming her features from desperate to almost predatory.

"Tilt your head," she commands, and I comply without hesitation, exposing the junction where my neck meets my shoulder.

She rises on her toes, her breath hot against my skin. There's a moment of anticipation, a heartbeat where everything seems to pause.

Then her teeth sink into my flesh.

Pain blazes through me, sharp and electric, radiating from the bite in white-hot waves. I gasp, my hands instinctively tightening on her waist.

It hurts—more than I expected—but beneath the pain is something else, something warm and viscous and golden that spreads through my veins like honey.

Evelyn holds the bite, a growl rumbling in her chest as her teeth press deeper.

I feel skin break, taste copper in the back of my throat, though it's not my mouth that's bleeding.

Then, just as suddenly as it began, the pain transforms. It melts into pleasure so intense I have to bite back a moan. Heat rushes through me, pooling in my stomach, my groin, the base of my spine. My vision blurs at the edges, narrowing until all I can see, all I can sense, is Evelyn.

And then the bond link crashes into me. A speargun, made of gingerbread, shoots right through my heart that pulls me to her, colliding our bodies, connecting them.

Her eyes water and soften with a look of love I don't think anyone has ever held for me before.

Suddenly, impossibly, I can feel her—not just her physical presence, but something deeper, more essential. I feel her desire, her fear, her desperate need to keep me close. It's overwhelming, disorienting, and the most profoundly intimate thing I've ever experienced.

And I know in this instant, she won't regret it. Because now we are one, and I truly, truly know what she wants.

Evelyn releases the bite, her tongue darting out to lap at the wound. The gentle pressure sends another bolt of pleasure-pain through me, and I can't stop the shudder that runs down my spine.

She pulls back, her eyes meeting mine. There's a new awareness in her gaze, a recognition. She feels it too—this connection, this bond, this invisible thread now binding us together.

"There," she says, her voice husky. She reaches up to touch the mark, her fingers gentle. "Now you can go. But come right back."

I nod, still too stunned to speak. The bond thrums between us, new and raw and potent.

I lean down and press my lips to hers, a brief, gentle kiss that somehow expresses more than any kiss I've ever given before. "I'll be right back," I promise against her mouth.

She nods, eyes bright with unshed tears. "You better be. Or you're fired..." She looks bashful and adds, "as my assistant. Not my beta."

CHAPTER 5
Finn

The hallway stretches before me, familiar in a way that makes my skin prickle. I know that the next door on the left leads to a small kitchenette where developers grab coffee and decompress.

I know the door after that is a supply closet.

I know these things the way you know the layout of your own home—a deep, instinctual knowledge that bypasses conscious thought.

I've seen this all. I've been here.

I stop at the kitchenette door, hesitating before pushing it open. If I'm wrong—if there's no kitchenette—then maybe I can still cling to the comforting fiction that I'm having some sort of breakdown. That would be easier to accept than...whatever this is.

The door swings open: a kitchenette. Just as I knew it would be.

The same white cabinets, the same blue mugs hanging from hooks. I step inside, drawn by some perverse need to confirm what I already know.

The note. If it's there, then this is real.

I open the fridge. And it's there. Just as I knew it would be.

On the left, atop a stack of omega yogurts, all with the name "Samuel" sharpied to them, is a note proclaiming:

"There's only one omega named Samuel who works here, and you are not he! DO NOT EAT!"

I stumble back from the fridge, bumping into the table I knew was behind me, but slam into anyway.

It's real. It's real.

A few days ago, I followed Evelyn around this office as she did her last rounds of intimidating mingling before everyone left for the holidays. She sneered at the Christmas decorations that employees embellished their desks with, silently signalling her disapproval and wearing her disdain for the holiday like armor. She passed by, and they whispered, worried she'd fire them for the criminal offenses of "having a heart" and "showing a little Christmas Spirit for fuck's sake."

She didn't. She won't. She never does.

What I could see and they couldn't was the face she hid from them, the tears that threatened to fall, when her back was to them.

Overwhelmed with her hatred of Christmas, she stormed in here, determined to eat her feelings, snatched one of those yogurts and ate it with the unrestrained hunger of a woman about to lose her shit. She hurled the empty cup into the nearby recycling and reached for another, freezing when her brain registered the note. She straightened herself, redonned her ice queen facade, and called Bob.

"Bobby, set up a weekly delivery of Omega Delight Probiotic Greek Yogurt to be stocked in all kitchenettes."

She paused. Then paced with the determined energy of a woman implementing a plan.

"Actually, let's start providing breakfast and lunch to all employees."

Pause.

"Uh. Huh. Yeah. You handle the logistics of how we decide what to stock, but make sure we have foods that support omegas during all phases of their heat cycles. Oh, take care of the betas and their menstrual phases, too. I don't know what male betas deal with—"

Pause.

Small laugh. "Good to know. Tell them HR is making us do it. Make something up."

Another pause.

"Thanks, Bobby. That's why I pay you the big bucks."

Pause.

"Yeah, bye."

When she hung up, she grabbed another yogurt and stormed out; the anger that had dissolved during her conversation with Bob returned.

This is insane.

I'm insane. Right?

It's not real. It can't be.

No. I'm not crazy. It's real.

If that's true, then the Evelyn I've been following is the real Evelyn.

Dream Evelyn is not a dream at all, but a real woman working in this building, unaware that some stranger has been witnessing her life for months. The thought makes me dizzy with possibilities, both thrilling and terrifying.

These aren't vague impressions; they're not lucky guesses or confirmation bias. These are intimate details about people I've never met and relationships I couldn't possibly know about, unless I really have been following Evelyn around, experiencing it myself—unless she and I are connected somehow, across distance, across logic, across the boundaries of what should be possible.

My hand goes to my thigh, to the patch, stuck uselessly there. My skin feels hot against my fingertips, almost burning, even through the pants—desperate for the pharmaceuticals that it relies on to suppress my alpha biology.

This isn't withdrawal.

This is real.

Everything about this place is real. More real than anything I've experienced in years. More real than my self-imposed isolation. More real than the careful barriers I've built between myself and the world.

I stumble back into the hallway on unsteady legs and lean against the wall, trying to regain control. My bags thud to the floor beside me, suddenly too heavy to carry. My heart hammers against my ribs.

The gingerbread intensifies, a warm wave making my knees weaker. My alpha instincts, long suppressed by chemicals and sheer force of will, stir in response.

It's real. Not in my head.

She's close. Evelyn is close.

The gingerbread hooks into something primal in my hindbrain, tugging me to where I know she is—like a fish on a line.

My breathing quickens, shallow pants that don't bring enough oxygen. Black spots dance at the edges of my vision.

I rub the back of my neck. The scent-suppressing patches roll at the corner. I rip them off. I run my hand through my hair, removing my hood.

I leave my bags. I don't need them.

My feet carry me forward, through the open floor plan, on a path etched into my memory by experiences. Motion-activated lights blink on in my wake as if they're encouraging me, watching me, just as excited as I am to see my love story unfold.

I am coming, my love.

Left at the end of this hallway. Right at the water cooler. Past the wall of employee photos where Evelyn's picture shows her not smiling, not quite frowning, a perfect encapsulation of her perpetually unimpressed demeanor.

The gingerbread scent pulls me onward, stronger with each step.

Her office is just ahead. I know it the way birds know north, a compass needle in my soul pointing unerringly toward her. I turn the corner, and there it is—the photo wall exactly as I knew it would be, and Evelyn's glassed office.

I freeze, stunned by the gravity of the moment. A flush of heat starts in my core and radiates outward.

"Evelyn," I breathe her name, the sound barely more than an exhale.

Something shifts in the air: a subtle change in pressure like the moment before lightning strikes. The gingerbread scent sharpens, cutting through everything else, unmistakably Evelyn. Unmistakably my omega.

My omega.

But not just my omega: Preston. Chris. Tim.

I know them.

They're guarding Evelyn. Protecting her.

Good.

But wait…they're protecting her from what?

I inhale, deeper.

Me? Ha. Good luck with that.

I take another step forward, drawn by a force stronger than my fear.

Where's Bob?

My head whips toward where I came. He's looking for me. I can smell him.

But I can't focus on him. Can't focus on anything except the truth that's finally, undeniably clear: my dreams haven't been dreams at all.

They've been real.

Evelyn is real.

I don't care about anything except reaching her, seeing her with my own eyes, confirming with all my senses what my heart already knows. Tears spring from my eyes, hot and sudden—overwhelmed, relieved.

Not crazy.

Fate.

Love.

Real.

I run toward the door, my feet moving on their own accord, rushing me toward the woman that even time and space couldn't keep me away from.

I'm coming, my love!

CHAPTER 6
Preston

Her body locks around my knot like we've been doing this our whole lives, not just this afternoon. The tremors of Evelyn's orgasm ripple through us both, and her fingers leave streaks down my "slutty forearms," as she calls them.

She goes limp against me, a puppet with cut strings, but I hold her steady, hands gentle on her hips. The gingerbread scent of her softens from desperate to content, and my hot chocolate responds in kind, a dog following its owner's cues.

The moment Bob left, Evelyn pushed me back to the nest to finish what she started with me—destroying what remained of our clothing. I don't mind. She can use me to her heart's content because it contents my heart. But now, the two of us are locked together, alone in the nest, nuzzling into each other—just the two of us.

Chris hovers by the door, guarding it, exuding an anxiety that is so overwhelming it's almost a cock block—almost. Tim, who moments ago was whispering in Evelyn's ears, rubbing her clit, and singing her praises, is at Chris's side, fueling his anxiety with nervous pacing. But me, I'm just here, knot-locked in my girl, happy as a clam that I get her all to myself right now.

Speaking of clams, I'm feeling kind of clammy.

Actually, I'm not feeling too well at all.

Evelyn turns her head, resting on my shoulder.

"Hey, Preston. I'm sorry," she says, voice rough. "For being so... possessive earlier. I had no right."

I lean down and nuzzle the nape of her neck. "It's okay. I understand omegas can get possessive during heat." I press my lips to the shell of her ear, feel her shiver. "Actually, I find it flattering."

She almost fights me on the heat thing. I see her lips curl in the way they always do when she screams "pre-heat," but instead, she snorts, "You would."

I laugh, lean forward, and kiss her. "I get it, babygirl. There's a steady little voice in the back of my head that wants to murder the rest of these guys to keep you to myself." I grin over at Tim and Chris. They look slightly offended, so I add, "But I'm not gonna! Obviously."

Tim finally stops his nervous pacing—that was actually making me dizzy now that I think about it. "Gee, thanks, Pres," he says, leaning against her desk.

I beam. "Thank your scents. I smell you all and realize I like you too much to kill you."

They don't seem relieved, probably because they aren't afraid of me, which is fine. I know I can kill them if I want, and that's all that matters. It's easier when you're not suspected, anyway.

Still leaning in, I whisper so only Evelyn can hear, "But just barely too much to kill them."

She giggles. Actually giggles. It's like crystal bells tinkling. It transforms her face into something softer, younger.

"Did you just giggle?" I ask, surprised, smitten.

"No," she says, but she's still smiling.

"Sure."

She shifts, "You know, you're the first alpha I ever actually considered my friend. I know you were a client, but..."

The admission catches me off guard. I'm flattered, and strangely moved. "Really?"

"All those virtual meetings," she continues. "You never tried to tell me how to run my company. You never mansplained game design to me. Never alphasplained finances to me. You just...respected me."

Worshipped is more like it. "Well, you're fucking brilliant at what you do. Why would I tell you how to do it?"

She laughs again, a real laugh this time. "You'd be surprised how many alphas, especially the male ones, think they can."

"Well, I don't know if you noticed, but...I kind of like being told what to do," I say, kissing her shoulders.

"I think I'm getting that impression, yes," she giggles again.

"It's funny, huh? How being told what to do makes you rage, but it gives me a raging hard-on."

This time, she laughs so deeply it vibrates through my knot.

"Yeah, like we're opposites attracting or something."

"I tried to ask you out so many times...you know, I...the only reason I'm in this city right now is I was hoping I'd get the courage to finally ask you out."

"I guess it's good for us that the build didn't work then."

"So, I have something I need to admit. I saw what you were watching on your phone."

She looks up, embarrassed for a split second, then says, "Well, I guess I've done significantly more embarrassing things since then."

I clear my throat so that when she tears it out, it won't soil her. "And when I saw that, I thought you might be in heat. So, I came here hoping...God, I sound like a fucking creep. I'm not sure what came over me. I convinced myself my patch would stop this from happening, but—"

"I always wanted to fuck you," she says with a grin.

"You gonna be mad at me when your heat passes?"

She sighs. "I feel like I should be, but...I don't think I will. My heat is supposed to start in the New Year, so ask me after that." She smirks.

I laugh, "Alright, I will."

She rests her head on my shoulder, and I kiss the top of her head.

Struck by a sudden desire to have her know everything about me, I say, "I was so nervous to meet you. I knew you were the omega for me, but this morning all I could think of was how I was going to fuck it up somehow."

"How'd you get over it?"

"My packmates," I respond, then add, "platonic packmates," not wanting to set off another wave of fury. "They're always talking me off ledges. But I'm trying this whole thing where I'm living in the present. And right now, the present is pretty perfect. Want to see a picture?"

She nods, curious.

I glance around, spot my pants, well, what's left of them, crumpled in the corner where they landed during our earlier frenzy. Moving my head around makes me a bit dizzy. I should probably eat something.

"Hey, Tim," I say, getting his attention. "Umm, could you grab my phone and that alpha power bar out of my pants pocket for me?" Tim unfolds himself from the bundle of anxiety he's standing in and retrieves the alpha bar and phone without question. He passes them over with the polite efficiency of a man who's used to following instructions.

I swipe open the photos app. I'm proud of the fact that I don't have to pass through any embarrassing selfies or dick pics to get to the one I want to show her.

"Can I see?" Tim asks, leaning in over Evelyn's shoulder.

"Yeah. Here," I say, showing them a group shot of my pack from last Christmas—the five of us in matching sweaters, mugging for the camera.

"That's Felix, Talia, Derek, and Ben," I say, pointing them out. "We were in a sitcom together as kids. It ran for six seasons on ABO Fami—"

Chris lights up like a fucking Christmas tree and says, "Wait...wait. Are you talking about *That's a Bunch*? You're in a pack with Talia Sync!?" He leaves his perch by the door and barrels over to see the phone. He leans in over Tim's shoulders to see, practically folding Tim in half.

I grin at him, oddly pleased. "Yeah, I am."

"I always had a bit of a crush on Talia. She was so edgy and cool." Chris smiles, returning to his station near the door, and for a moment, he looks younger, less intense. Tim grins at him, looking a bit smitten.

I laugh at how exactly opposite her type he is, but I don't mention it. "I'll introduce you. I'm sure we'll all be spending a lot of time together, now that—" I say, pointing at my knot locked into Evelyn, who smiles sleepily.

So cute.

Evelyn bites her lip, "And you're platonic?"

Aww, my sweet little omega is still jealous.

I nuzzle into her, marking her with my scent and letting her know I'm not going anywhere. "Yeah. My pack is family, but we're not... sexually compatible. And I've never met an omega who felt like mine. Until now."

She melts, wrapping her legs and arms tighter around me.

I continue, "Now they essentially work for me." I point them out again, "Talia is my stylist; Felix does hair and makeup; Ben is my assistant; Derek is my energy and endocrinology alignment coach. Ben and Derek are a bonded pair."

Evelyn laughs again, and I wish I could bottle the sound. "Derek is your what?"

My vision goes black around the edges. "Huh? What was that, babygirl? Sorry, I'm not feel—I should probably eat something."

Chris squints at me, scrutinizing me as if he's never seen me before. "Preston, when was the last time you've eaten?"

I try to tear the alpha bar open, but my fingers are refusing to work.

I attempt a smile, but it's surprisingly hard. "Haven't eaten all day... so, like, 8 p.m."

Chris actually removes himself from the door to approach me, worry wracking his face. He practically yells at me, "You what!? Are you insane!? You can't rut on an empty stomach. You'll kill yourself." Chris grabs the alphabar I'm fumbling with and rips it open for me.

I bite into the bar and say through chews, "Wasn't planning on rutting today." *Well, maybe a little.*

"I wasn't either," Chris mutters. "You shouldn't have taken your patch off," he says, feeling my forehead with the back of his hand. "Fuck, Preston. A rut burns through calories like a wildfire." He stands looking around anxiously. "Isn't there a fridge in here somewhere, Tim?"

Tim nods.

"Can you get him some food. Anything with calories." He returns his attention to me. "Preston, rutting at your age is dangerous enough."

"Hey, I'm not that old—"

"You will literally give yourself a heart attack."

"Die doing what I love, am I right?" I joke, but it comes out flat, because I am starting to feel like I might die.

Tim opens a hidden door amongst the walls, revealing a sleek refrigerator. "All that's in here is some water. There's a kitchenette, but it probably doesn't have much. Maybe some yogurt. It got mostly cleaned out for the holidays."

Chris takes the alpha bar from me, tears it open further, and returns it like a momma chimp peeling a banana for her baby. I take another bite, and it makes me feel a little better.

Thanks, Derek.

Tim pulls out his phone. "I can order some food."

"Yeah, let's do that. Get protein. Lots of it. And complex carbs." He stares ahead and checks his finger in the air as he lists out items, as if the list is visible to only him. "Salmon, brown rice, sweet potatoes. Nuts and dried fruits for quick energy." He looks between the three of us. "Get at least forty servings."

Tim is on his phone, scrolling with the focused intensity of a man on a mission.

"What? Why so much? Bulking us up for a superalpha role?" I ask, amused.

He gives me a look that's half doctor, half alpha. "You've never been through an omega's heat before, have you?"

I shrug. "No."

"Then trust me on this. When her heat really kicks in—"

I interrupt, "Wait! So, that whole 'pre-heat' thing wasn't a bit? I thought she was just being stubborn."

"I'm not stubborn!" she says, waking up, eyes still heavy as she fights sleep. "I'm determined."

"So determined, babygirl," I say, petting her head as she lays it back down on my shoulder.

Chris meets my gaze, steady, serious, looking like a man prepared for battle. "What she's experiencing now is just Act 1."

Evelyn's eyes are closed, and she's smiling just a little. I can feel her appreciation that he doesn't insist her heat has already started, even though we all know it has. It's the respect in the fiction that matters to her.

He mouths since her eyes are closed, "NOT PRE HEAT—ACTUAL HEAT." Then he says aloud, since she can hear, "When it peaks, moments like this, where she's lucid and sleepy, will be few and far between. I honestly don't think the two of us are going to be enough. Tim and Bob can help...but..." He sighs. "Shit—this is going to be rough—"

Chris stands and looks at Tim, waffling as he decides what to do. "We'll order food, but you need to rest while you can. Don't knot her again until after you've eaten."

"Yes, doctor," I say, not disagreeing, but it sounds sarcastic anyway.

Tim finishes placing the order and announces, "Food will be here in forty minutes."

"Alright," Chris says. "Once Bob gets back from getting rid of this Finn guy, let's talk to him about how he planned to ride this out. Ideally, we'll eat and then get her to her real nest. Not just for her—all of us. An office isn't a suitable location. We need access to a shower—"

I perk up, but only slightly, "Oh, a shower would be really nice. I feel...sticky."

Evelyn stirs and whines, eyes still closed, "I knew it! Preston! You don't love me. You want to wash me off."

"Oh, no, babygirl, it's these other fools I want to wash off." Then I whisper, "Especially that big dummy, Chris." I lie down with her, tucking her into her nest and holding her tight.

"Yeah. Big dummy," she smirks and then falls back asleep.

Chris looks at me, wounded.

"Hey buddy, I didn't make the hierarchy, she did." I wrap my arms around her, determined to move up the ladder and usurp Tim.

Well, I might as well get some rest.

My eyes drift closed, perfectly content, but that's when I feel it, snapping my eyes open.

A shift in the air, like the atmospheric pressure dropping before a storm. Everyone in the room tenses simultaneously. Evelyn's scent sharpens with confusion, and the hairs on the back of my neck stand up.

"What was that?" Tim asks, voicing what we're all thinking.

Chris moves to the door and peers through the glass panel's blinds. His massive frame goes rigid.

"Fuck," he says, voice flat.

"What is it? What's happening!?" I ask, frantic, unable to move, still locked into Evelyn.

Chris turns, his expression a strange mix of resignation and anticipation. "I found Finn Future. He's...he's gone full rut, running full speed toward the door."

CHAPTER 7
Evelyn

My eyes snap open as an invisible thread pulls taut behind my sternum and yanks me toward the door. A presence, a scent, ripples through the air like a plucked string, vibrating against my skin, crawling into my nose, and flooding my brain with candy canes. Peppermint so sharp it cuts through the fog of my sleep, slicing away the drowsiness and replacing it with a singular, desperate need.

My body moves before my brain catches up.

I lurch forward and gasp as Preston's knot holds me in place.

Preston's arms, still wrapped around me, tighten reflexively as the invisible thread hooks deeper into my gut, jerking me toward the door and tugging with the persistence of destiny. His knot twitches, reminding me that it's locked inside me, but even that isn't enough to keep me here.

Not now.

Not when that scent is calling.

Preston whimpers—actually whimpers—against my neck. It's not that needy whimper he does during sex, but the whimpering fear of an alpha being truly forced into submission. "What is that? What's happening?" he asks, his voice cracking slightly.

I don't answer.

I can't.

Words feel unnecessary, clumsy things.

The only thing that matters is opening the door and reaching the source of that scent that's been haunting me, protecting me, loving me, all day—maybe longer...I just can't recall...

Candy cane. Mine.

I untangle myself from Preston, his knot finally receding enough that I can slip free with a small squeeze and tug. The sensation is almost painful—an emptiness—that my heat screams, "Fill with a knot!"

But the emptiness doesn't matter.

Nothing matters.

Just candy cane. Just him.

I'm standing, swaying.

Every cell in my body screams that I need to open that door. Right. Now. Like there's a giant magnet on the other side and I'm nothing but iron filings, helpless against its force.

Door.

Now.

Go.

Fuck.

Breed.

Tim scrambles toward me. "Evie, what are you doing?" His voice is thin with worry. "You should rest."

His words barely register. All I know is that something—someone—is on the other side of that door, and every second that passes feels like torture.

"I need to—" My voice sounds foreign to my own ears, breathy and desperate. I take a step toward the door, ignoring the wetness tracking down my thighs and the trembling in my knees.

Preston is suddenly behind me, hands on my shoulders. "Babygirl, you can rest, we'll see who it is," he says, trying to sound calm but achieving something closer to desperation. *This guy got nominated for an Oscar?*

Preston adds, "You're naked. It could be anyone."

But it's not 'anyone.' It's who I've been looking for my whole life. I know this fact as surely as I know my own name.

I shake my head, my vision blurring at the edges.

Someone grabs me, says something.

I ignore him, taking a step toward the door.

Another voice.

Another hand. Two hands. Gripping me. Stopping me.

"Let me go," I manage—the words scraped raw from my throat.

Chris's massive frame stands between me and the exit, arms spread wide like he's guarding a goal. "Evelyn," he says, his tone maddeningly reasonable, "you're in heat. You shouldn't—"

"Move," I say, with murderous intent.

My gingerbread spikes, thick, angry, fogging the world, squeezing under the door to find its match on the other side.

I feel it—the candy cane—as the tendrils of my gingerbread hold it.

Penetrate nostrils. He can smell me. Just like I can smell him. We are already one. Molecules of me float in his lungs.

Tim steps between me and the door, hands raised in placation. "Evie, please. Your heat—"

"My heat is my business," I snap. "Get out of my way!" I shout, pushing past him.

He stumbles back, surprised by the force. Adrenaline powers me, giving me the strength I need to get to the safety of my mate.

My mate. My alpha. My fate.

He's on the other side of the door.

I know it. I do.

"Evelyn, please let us check," Preston says, and his voice is almost enough to make me hesitate.

Almost.

Chris doesn't budge when I reach him. His face is a mask of alpha concern, green eyes dark with worry. "Evelyn," he says, voice low, "I can't let you do this. Not when you're not thinking clearly."

Nothing has ever been more clear. The answers to all the universe's questions are on the other side of that door. He's standing right outside the door, just waiting for me to open it for him.

"I am thinking perfectly clearly," I snarl, trying to duck under his arm.

He shifts, blocking me again.

Preston crowds behind me, his scent sharp with protective instinct. "Let's all just take a breath," he says, but I can hear the tremor in his voice. He's scared. But I'm not. I know that what is on the other side of the door is the one thing in the universe I never have to be afraid of.

I can feel him waiting. He's calling to me. He could kick in the door so easily, but he doesn't. He's waiting for me.

I try to push past Chris again, but he plants his feet wider.

"Move," I repeat, digging my nails into my palms to keep from scratching him.

"Evelyn," Chris says, "I know what's best for you right now."

That does it. My vision goes red at the edges. "You don't know shit about what's best for me." I push against him, but it's like shoving a mountain. His chest doesn't give an inch.

Chris plants his feet firmer, "You need to—"

"STOP FUCKING TELLING ME WHAT TO DO!!" I howl.

This fucking guy never learns.

The pull gets stronger, more insistent. No longer a tug, but a full-body ache, like my skin is two sizes too small.

My heart hammers against my ribs, a trapped bird desperate for flight.

I glare at Chris, make like I'm going to say something, but instead I move around him, fluid and fast in a way that surprises these lumbering blockheads.

"She's going feral," Chris says, "We have to stop her."

"STOP UNDERESTIMATING ME, YOU GIANT FUCKING ASSHOLE! I played lacrosse in college! I'm not feral! I'm spritely!"

My limbs should be shaky, my coordination shot. But I'm moving with a strength and purpose that seems to come from somewhere outside myself.

Fueled by my love's scent.

My alpha. Prime Alpha. He lifts me up. He doesn't hold me down.

"We can't let her out there. Neither of them are in their right minds," Chris says, as if I can't fucking hear him. The condescension in his voice would normally piss me off, but right now I can't spare the energy to be angry.

Not when I'm so close.

The door.

I have to open it.

I just need to get to it.

Tim lunges for me, but I sidestep him.

Chris makes a grab for my arm, and I duck.

Wave after wave of candy cane seeps through the cracks of the door, calling me, encouraging me, loving me.

Preston tries to circle around, to cut me off, but I twist away, my nakedness and slick making me slippery and impossible to catch.

I lead them to my nest, as far away from the door as the room will allow. The big, stupid idiots think they can corner me, but that's all the space I need to reach the door unobstructed.

Ha, there's a benefit to being a tiny slippery omega after all.

I reach the door, the last obstacle between me and destiny, and fling it open with zero hesitation, uncaring about my nudity. The scent hits me full in the face—a wall of peppermint so intense it knocks the air from my lungs and the gingerbread from my glands.

And the world stops.

Everything condenses to a single point and expands outward. Universes are destroyed and remade. All existence blinks out then reappears.

My knees buckle, but I don't fall.

He's there.

He's right there.

Tall, impossibly beautiful. White hair. Dressed in black. A skeletal smile painted on a black mask.

He gasps. Hit with the shock, too. And I recognize him.

I don't know him.

But I'd know him anywhere.

I know him.

The candy cane scent pours off him in waves, mixing with my gingerbread, creating something new and perfect and terrifyingly familiar.

A white hot static overtakes my brain as all my neurons click into a new place. Each connection rewiring itself, morphing, creating this new Evelyn: the one who knows; the one who sees; the one who found.

Mine! He's mine.

Beautifully, perfectly, always mine.

Always has been.

He's tall—taller than Preston, almost as tall as Chris—with white-blond hair falling in waves to his shoulders, pushed back from his forehead where sweat has dampened it. He's breathing hard, chest heaving under a simple black t-shirt that clings to him like a second skin. He's wearing a black hoodie, track pants, and a medical mask that covers his lower face with a skull smile.

For a moment, we just stare at each other. His eyes are wild, pupils blown wide with the milky white hue of an alpha fully consumed by rut. But the clouds wipe away, revealing big, beautiful brown eyes now clear with recognition—the same knowing that's burning through me. He looks at me like I'm the answer to every question he's ever asked.

"Finn," I breathe. "You're real."

Mine. Mine. Mine.

I don't consciously decide to move. My body simply recognizes its other half and acts accordingly. I propel myself forward, desperate to be in his arms, to press my face into his neck and breathe him in until I drown in peppermint—until his teeth rip through my flesh and we are truly one.

So perfect. My everything. My reason for being an omeg—

"EVELYN, STOP," Chris roars, his voice dropping into that register that only alphas can reach—the voice that makes atoms stop vibrating, that makes gravity pause, that makes omegas freeze in their tracks and betas submit. The alpha bark—a deeper, rougher voice infused with an authority that bypasses logic and latches directly onto my subconscious.

The command slams into me like a physical blow. My body freezes mid-step, muscles locking up against my will, breath catching in my lungs.

I'm motionless—a statue carved of hate. Rage floods my system. White-hot fury, all-consuming, erupts in my chest.

How dare he?

HOW FUCKING DARE HE use his alpha bark on me?

The heat-fog clears for a moment as wrath burns through it.

I'm not some mindless omega bitch to be commanded.

I'm not something to be controlled.

I can't move.

Frozen.

The moment I can move, I'm ripping his fucking windpipe from his throat. *Let's see him bark at me after that.*

How dare he do this to me!!!??

Tears well in my eyes as my anger transforms into intense, overwhelming sadness.

How could he? How could he still...after everything that's happened... think he has any right to control me? After everything we talked about, after I made it crystal clear that I need autonomy, that I need respect, that I need to be seen as a person and not just an omega—and he does this?

Finn moves, lightning fast. He's a blur of motion, closing the distance between us with a speed that shouldn't be possible. When his body slams into mine, it's as if every sensation I've ever felt up to this moment was a ghost of a sensation in comparison.

His arms tighten around me, and his eyes stay locked on my face. "It's okay, my love. I got you. Are you okay?" he asks me, voice like thunder wrapped in velvet, completely ignoring Chris, ignoring everything but me, and stroking my hair.

And just like that, the invisible force holding me in place vanishes.

I don't think. I don't plan. I just move.

I launch myself at him. My arms wrap around his neck, my legs around his waist, before I even realize I've moved.

He catches me effortlessly, like he knew I was coming, like he's been waiting for me his whole life. One hand grips my thigh, supporting my weight as if I'm nothing, the other tangles in my hair.

Safe, happy, perfect, and—

Chris takes a step toward us. "Get away from her," he growls.

"NO! You get away!" I yell.

Chris freezes as if I had an alpha bark. Finn doesn't even acknowledge Chris; he simply looks at me. I am the sun, and his eyes are planets that revolve around me.

I'm shaking with rage, teeth bared, a growl building in my throat that would make others back away if they actually respected omegas. "You," I hiss at Chris, "do not command me. You do not own me!"

Chris, still firm in his belief that he has the right to control me if it's what he deems is for my own good, says, "Evelyn, I'm sorry, I had to—"

I spit, "Fuck. You."

Finn pulls down his mask, revealing a face so perfect it hurts to look at—high cheekbones, full lips, the kind of beauty that doesn't seem quite real. His jaw is sharp enough to cut glass. He's stunning in the figurative and literal sense—I'm literally stunned, unable to speak.

His eyes find mine, and his gaze is so soft that it makes my chest ache. "My love," he says, breaking the armor around my heart. It cracks into two pieces and falls at his feet.

"He used his alpha bark on me, Finn," I whisper, as if I've known him my whole life. "How could he do that to me?"

My eyes water.

Something dark and dangerous flashes in Finn's eyes at the sight of my tears.

Chris straightens. He doesn't address me. Alpha addressing alpha. "She wasn't thinking clearly. I was trying to protect—"

Finn finally turns to look at the others, acknowledging their presence for the first time. "LET HER DO WHAT SHE WANTS," Finn roars, his alpha bark so powerful it seems to shake the foundations of the building.

His voice. God, his voice.

It's not just an alpha bark—it's something more, something primal and ancient that makes the air vibrate. It reverberates through the air, through my chest, through the very foundation of the building.

The command isn't directed at me, but I feel it nonetheless, a ripple of pure, dominant energy. Somehow, it makes me feel stronger, energized, not paralyzed like every other alpha bark I've heard. It's like it was made to support me, not subdue me.

And just like that, all three men—Chris, Preston, and Tim—drop to their knees. Not fighting it, not hesitating. They just...kneel. Even Chris, with all his imposing size, sinks to the floor as if Finn stood behind him and kicked his knees forward.

They submit. Fully. Exposing their throats. To my alpha. To our alpha. To Prime Alpha.

Finn looks back at me, as if he couldn't care less about them. His face softens instantly when his eyes meet mine again. All the fierceness in his face softens into something that makes my heart stutter. His eyes are so gentle, so reverent, that tears prick at the corners of my eyes.

"Hey," he says, voice gentle now. "Are you okay?"

"Yes," I whisper, unable to say much more, still stunned by the beauty of this man.

He says so softly, voice still so deliciously deep, but at a whisper just for me. "It's okay, my love. I'll never let anyone try to control you again."

His mouth finds mine, and the world narrows to this single point of contact. His lips are soft but insistent, tasting of mint and promise, claiming me with a thoroughness that makes my head spin. The kiss deepens, and I whimper into his mouth, my fingers tangling in his hair, pulling him closer, closer.

Closer. Closer. Closer.

Mine. Mine. Mine.

When we break apart, both gasping for air, he presses his forehead to mine. "My love. My everything," he murmurs.

I should be terrified. I should be backing away from this stranger who just commanded my pack to their knees with a single word. I should be calling security. Instead, I whisper, "Take me to my nest."

He doesn't hesitate. He adjusts his grip on me, hoisting me higher against him, his smile breaking like the sun through the storm of my anger, and walks toward my nest.

CHAPTER 8
Evelyn

He carries me like I'm an extension of himself, like I'm a weight he's carried his whole life. My legs are locked around his waist, and his hands are steady under my thighs.

The others still kneel. Their eyes track us, and they turn, exposing their necks, to Finn as we walk past, but Finn doesn't spare them another glance. I'm the only thing in the world. I feel their eyes on us, but I can't bring myself to care.

Not now.

Not when Finn is carrying me to my nest.

Not when his scent is wrapping around me like a blanket and the hard length of him is pressing against me through his clothes.

All that matters is our coupling.

"My love," he says, the words breathed against my lips, "I'm here. I'm finally with you. I can't believe I'm finally able to touch you."

I whisper, "I feel like...you've been with me for so long."

"I have," he says against my lips, his voice cracking with emotion. "I've been with you every day since we signed the *Torchbearer* contract."

"What do you mean?"

"You couldn't sense me, but I was here. I could see you, hear you, smell you," he inhales. "I just couldn't touch you. I've lain next to you, stood next to you, every day, unable to touch you."

"How?" I whisper against his neck, breathing in his scent.

"I don't know."

"So, earlier...in my chair? On my desk? That was you?"

There's a moment of panic in his eyes, like he thinks I'll yell or scream. *I'd never yell at you, you perfect creature.* He says, voice like silk, "Yes. I—I thought you were a dream. I thought I was going crazy."

"I thought you were a dream! I thought heat had me hallucinating the ghost of a boy bander rutting into me," I say, my heart pounding in my chest.

"I—" His steps falter, just for a moment, wariness flickering across his face, as if he doesn't want me to recognize him.

"You are Zane from Fates Five, aren't you?"

He nods and looks down. "Yes."

I laugh, the sound shaky with need and disbelief. "This is amazing... Your music..." I trail off, suddenly shy, and trying to hold in my inner fangirl.

He nuzzles my hair, his voice a low rumble against my ear. "My music, what? You can tell me anything, my love."

I grab his face and kiss him again. "During my first heat, Tim played the *Omegababy* album on loop for me..."

His arms tighten around me, a small growl escaping his throat. "Did he, now?"

"Yes. That album, that song, always makes me feel better during my heat. It's stupid, but...I would pretend that song was written just for me." I'm sobbing, kissing him.

"It was, my love, I just didn't know it until now," he whispers back, kissing me, holding me, completing me. "Everything has been for you. I'm happy that it could help you."

Finn lays me down with a gentleness that makes my eyes sting. He follows me down, covering my body with his, his weight a delicious pressure.

Finn—Zane—THNTS.exe—whatever name he goes by now—holds me tighter, burying his face in my neck. "My love," he says, the words vibrating through me, "I've waited so long to touch you."

He props himself on his elbows, looking down at me with a reverence that makes me squirm, and strokes my hair back from my forehead. "You're so beautiful," he says, with such gentleness I could melt into this nest, a happy little omega.

My heat, always a dreadful moment ruining cunt, comes roaring back with renewed intensity. A cramp rips through me, sharp and unexpected.

I gasp, arching against Finn. I cling to him, burying my face in his neck, breathing in his scent like it's oxygen.

"Shh," he soothes, "I've got you, my love." He strokes my hair back from my face, again.

I clutch at his hoodie, desperate to feel his skin.

"Please," I whimper. "I need—"

"I know," he says, his voice dropping lower. "I've been with you for a long time. I know what you need."

And he does. He knows exactly what I need. In this moment, I need gentleness, I need care, I need consolation, and that's what he gives me.

He purrs, but not just a purr—a purr wrapped in a melodic hum. The vibration travels from his chest to mine, where we're pressed together. The sound soothes something deep within me, easing the cramp, making me melt against him.

And then, to my astonishment, he sings, "Babygirl, your love calls for me. You're pullin' at my heart from across the sea. Omegababy." And the song, just like always, melts the ice building in my veins and cools the magma in my core. It's as if the song, his voice, his breath can penetrate me in a way no knot ever could—entering my muscles, my bones, my essence.

And before another cramp even hits, he pulls back, strips quickly, efficiently, revealing a body that's both familiar and new to me. I've seen him shirtless in music videos, on a poster in my room, but this—this is different. *This is for me.*

There's a tattoo along his ribs, not quite on his back, not quite on his side, written in black script, faded by time. I attempt to read it, but I can only make out one word: "fox." Because before I can inspect it further, he's fully naked above me, magnificent and hard and perfect.

There's no hesitation when he covers my body with his. His hands slide up my thighs, and in the same motion, he aligns himself, the blunt head of his cock pressing against me only a moment before he slides into me with a groan that sounds like relief.

It's not like it was with the others. There's no resistance, no adjustment period, no hesitation. He fits me perfectly, like we were designed for each other. Like our bodies remember each other.

He pushes in slowly, stretching me, filling me, and resumes singing, his voice catching on the high notes as I clench around him. "Babygirl, your fever is back. And if I'm not enough, we'll form a pack. Omegababy."

Our eyes lock, and in his I see a lifetime of waiting, of searching, of knowing something was missing. I see the same hunger that's been gnawing at me, the same loneliness.

A cramp tries to build, but as he fills me completely, it's replaced by a pleasure so intense it borders on pain.

I wrap my legs around him, urging him deeper. "Finn," I gasp as he starts to move, his hips driving forward in a movement that matches the rhythm of the song.

He kisses me, his hands everywhere—in my hair, on my breasts, gripping my hips.

His eyes never leave mine as he continues to sing. His voice is a physical thing, wrapping around me like silk, easing the cramps, stoking the fire.

His fingers find the space between us, and he groans, breaking the melody. "God, you're perfect."

I reach for him, pull him down to me for a deep kiss.

His voice wraps around us both, a cocoon of sound and sensation.

I dig my nails into his back.

The candy cane scent of him is overwhelming now, mixing with my gingerbread until the whole nest smells like the cookies I made before everything changed. The cookies I made when I used to love Christmas. It smells like home, like everything I've been running from and everything I've been searching for.

Finn's eyes go white as rut fully overtakes him, but his pace and voice remain calm, worshipful. He doesn't rut into me; he continues to make love to me as if being with me, hugging me, loving me, kissing me, and singing to me is the most important thing in the world.

His knot swells, catching on my rim with each forward movement, the pressure building until finally, finally, the song reaches its climax, and so do I, crying out as waves of pleasure crash over me. "Babygirl, my heart was closed off. And if I'm out of line, you can be the boss. Omegababy."

Finn follows, his voice breaking on the final note as he shudders above me, inside me, his knot swelling and locking us together. The fullness, the perfect stretch of it, tips me over the edge again.

I come with his name on my lips. "Finn!" I moan, as my body clenches around his knot, milking him for everything he has to give.

He growls against my throat, the sound vibrating through my whole body. "Mine." I feel the scrape of his teeth, the promise of a bond.

"Yours," I agree, tilting my head to give him better access. "Always yours. Do it."

He sinks his teeth into my neck, and the pain is nothing compared to the pleasure that follows—a white-hot burst of sensation that ripples outward, consuming everything in its path.

I cry out, nails digging into his back, legs locked around his waist.

And then I'm falling, breaking apart, the orgasm washing through me in waves that seem endless.

Finn is still releasing his seed into me, triggering another wave of pleasure that has me seeing stars.

He collapses on top of me, careful to keep most of his weight on his forearms, his face buried in my neck where he's marked me. "I've looked for you," he whispers, his voice rough and broken. "My whole life, I've been looking for you."

I stroke his hair, his back, anywhere I can reach. "I'm here now," I tell him. "I'm here."

In the corner of my eye, I can see the others, watching us with expressions ranging from awe to confusion to something like acceptance.

CHAPTER 9

A jolt like touching a live wire stops me in my tracks, nearly doubling me over. Pain and pleasure fuse into a single white-hot sensation that shoots up my spine and explodes behind my eyes.

I gasp, falling back on my ass, vision suddenly filled with...Evelyn. I'm floating above her. I'm seeing through our pack bond, experiencing what she's experiencing.

Finn.

Her alpha.

My alpha.

Our alpha—Prime Alpha.

He's bonding with her.

Her neck is exposed, head thrown back, the line of her throat a perfect curve.

And then—teeth. Sharp canines sinking into tender flesh, blood beading around the puncture marks, and the raw, visceral surge of belonging that floods through the three of us.

The bond snaps into place like a key turning in a lock.

"Mine," a voice that isn't mine growls through my head.

Ours. Pack. Home.

The vision fades as quickly as it appeared, leaving me dazed and panting on the hallway floor. The ghost-sensation of Evelyn's skin, Finn's teeth against our skin, lingers.

A few moments ago, I was searching the development floor for Finn Future. Now I'm on the floor, coming in my pants.

"Holy shit," I whisper, scrambling to my feet. "She's bonded."

I run—really run this time, not the half-jog I've been doing in search of Finn, but an all-out sprint that has my lungs burning and legs screaming by the time I reach Evelyn's office. The door is still open, the scent of gingerbread and peppermint so thick it's like running face-first into a wall.

What I find inside stops me cold.

Evelyn is in her nest, eyes closed, with a look of perfect contentment on her face. Finn, who looks like the ghost of that pop star who disappeared when I was in high school, is wrapped around her, dwarfing her with his pale, massive frame, and tangling one hand in her hair.

They're locked together, his knot binding them in the most primal way possible, and there's blood—just a little—on her neck where he's marked her.

Chris, Preston, and Tim stand around the edges of the room, wrecked, like warriors just returned from the battlefield. Something seems to have drained the last bit of strength from them, and I don't think it was Evelyn's insatiable lust.

Chris leans against the wall, his usual tower of alpha grandeur diminished. His face is pale, and sweat beads on his forehead. Tim sits cross-legged on the floor nearby, staring at his hands as if they belong to someone else. Preston leans against the opposite wall, what clothes he still wears ripped to shreds, running his hand through his hair over and over, like he's trying to reset himself.

I walk in, slowly, careful not to wake Evelyn or draw the attention of the beautifully terrifying alpha she's locked onto. I join the others. "Jesus, you all look terrible," I say. I almost ask what's going on, but I certainly don't need to. I can see it for myself.

Preston attempts a smile, but it's a pale imitation of his usual charm. He wobbles a little, looking like he might pass out. Tim's stomach growls, followed immediately by Chris's. As if on cue, Finn's stomach rumbles so loudly it seems to shake the nest. He doesn't acknowledge it, doesn't even look our way. His entire focus is on Evelyn, with his fingers tracing patterns on her skin and his lips pressed to her temple. I realize I'm starving too—I've been running on adrenaline most of the day and didn't finish my salad.

And this is where I come in.

"Well, you're all going to need to eat," I say, taking mental inventory of what we have in the office kitchen: not enough.

"I ordered some food already," Tim says. "It should be here soon. I got enough for us all, but that was before—" he says, gesturing at Finn, who still hasn't even noticed I've walked into the room.

"Okay, great," I whisper. "After we all eat, we have to relocate to the nest at her house."

"We can't stay here?" Preston asks, slumping over.

"The office nest is fine for emergencies, but it's not equipped for a full heat. Especially not with a third alpha." I nod toward Finn. "It's just not going to be sustainable—we don't have the supplies, we don't have the facilities..." I sigh. "I've already got a whole team on standby, prepped to ensure her home nest is as comfortable as possible—not only for her, but anyone assisting her through the heat."

"How do we move her?" Preston asks, his movie-star face drawn with exhaustion.

"There's a specialized car service that transports omegas in heat with their nests and their rutting pack. I'll call them and—"

A soft whimper from the nest draws all our attention. Evelyn stirs. Her eyes flutter open, momentarily clear and focused in that brief window of lucidity between heat waves. She looks at Finn first—of course she does—her expression soft with wonder, then her gaze drifts to me.

"Bobby?" she calls, voice hoarse.

"Hey, boss," I say, trying not to convey the worry I'm feeling. "How are you feeling?"

She stretches, winces slightly, then smiles. "Like all my dreams just came true."

Finn chuckles, the sound deep and rumbling. His arms tighten around her possessively, as if he's a little kid who just had his favorite teddy returned to him.

"I'm happy for you, boss," I say and look at the rest of my pack. Evelyn is obviously my main priority, but now I have a responsibility to all of them. They are my pack. I am their beta. They need me. And right now they all look like they're about to keel over—even Finn, who sparkles with beauty, appears like some of his luster is dulled. I need them all at their best if they're going to take care of Evelyn.

"We need to get you home," I say, taking a tentative step closer. "To your real nest."

Her brow furrows, and she glances around the office nest, running her fingers over the blankets and pillows. She's still in a deep, dreamy state due to the bite, and I've never seen her so relaxed.

She yawns, "But I like this nest. You made it for me."

My chest tightens with affection. Even in the midst of her heat, even with her new alpha wrapped around her, she notices and appreciates what I've done.

"I made you an even better one at home," I explain gently. "It has all your favorite things. And it is soooo soft. But also, your alphas are all so big. They need more room and food if they can continue to please you to the best of their ability."

She should be practical about this, but practical is often a pipe dream with an omega in heat. She just pouts, shaking her head. "I don't want to go to that one," she mumbles, burrowing deeper into Finn's embrace.

"Why not, boss?"

"Because it reminds me of...them...my mean pack," she says, hiding her face in his chest.

The candy-caned rage that spills out of Finn is so intense I wouldn't be surprised if the whole city feels it. It's met with churning, burnt hot chocolate and a flaming Christmas tree amidst boiling snow. Spiced cranberries go sour, and even my cinnamon morphs to something more akin to salt. Then, the rumbling growls of three alphas, ready to commit acts of atrocity, vibrate through my head.

"I want to stay here." She looks up at me, eyes wide and soft in a way they only get during heat. "Please don't make me go home. My house still smells like them."

The growls are purrs now, the alphas' rage redirected to his true purpose: not murder and mutilation, but comforting their omega.

I gulp back my own rage. "Anything you want, boss. Don't worry. I'll take care of it."

"I knew I could count on you, Bobby," her eyes drift closed.

Time to get to work.

I turn from the nest. Finn's purr hits my back, gently pushing me forward, as if it's saying, "Go. Take care of our omega."

Chris approaches me, and he whispers, "Bob, what is the plan?"

The fact that he's asking me—that the big alpha doctor is deferring to me—would be more satisfying if I weren't so worried about her—about all of them.

I respond, "Ummm, okay, let me think for a minute..."

Alright, so we have three alphas and Tim. That might as well be four. But Chris is a brick house, so five...

I look at Finn.

Let's just call it six.

My calculations are interrupted with:

"Boooooooooobbbbyyyyyy!! I want you to come cuddle. I miss you." The naked need in her voice makes my throat close up.

I turn toward her instinctively and reach for her. But I hesitate, hand hovering just above her back and eyes darting to Finn. His focus is entirely on Evelyn, as if the rest of us barely exist, but I'm still not sure if he'll let me touch her.

Evelyn notices me looking at Finn. She beams at him, then turns that radiant smile on me. "Bobby, this is Finn. My alpha. Isn't he beautiful?" She says it with such pride, such certainty. Then she adds, "Finn, this is my Bobby. He's my bonded, too, my beta."

Finn's eyes flick to mine for the first time—intense brown irises that make me wonder if I'm as heterosexual as I thought I was. He doesn't speak to me, doesn't extend a hand, or make any typical greeting gesture. He simply doesn't rip my throat out and then returns his attention to Evelyn.

"Come," Evelyn says, patting the edge of the nest. "I need cuddles from my Bobby."

"Um, can I—"

He brushes his lips against her temple and murmurs, to her, not me, "Anything you want is yours, my love."

I guess that's permission.

I look toward the others. Chris looks down, jaw tight. Preston gives me an encouraging nod. Tim just looks worried, which is his default expression.

She is my everything. She is my world. And if I don't start making some calls soon, she is going to suffer. I cannot let that happen.

"Before I join you," I say, my body screaming to get in the nest and cuddle with them, but my mind reeling around the things I need to do to take care of her, "I just need to set some things in motion."

She pouts, but doesn't push.

I turn to Tim, who straightens under my attention. "Tim, go to my computer. There's a folder on the desktop labeled 'Evelyn's Heat.'"

Tim nods, already backing toward the door, clearly relieved to have a concrete task.

"There's a spreadsheet with a list of people we need to call. Go to the tab labeled 'In-Office Heat Contingency Plans.' It has the contact details for building security, food and water delivery, and a slew of other services we need to mobilize. All should already be on standby, but a few will need to be directed to the office instead of her home."

Tim nods, committing it to memory.

I bite my lip. I don't have time to explain the whole thing.

Fuck, should we do Contingency Plan A or B? Plan A accounts for alphas, but B accounts for—

"Bobby!" Evelyn whines, the sleepy contentment giving way to impatience. "Stop ignoring me!"

I turn back to find her pouting, eyes narrowed in that way that others find intimidating, but I've always found arousing.

Finn makes a low, soothing sound in his throat and whispers something in her ear that makes her melt against him. "My love," he says, loud enough for us to hear this time, "he's making sure those idiots take care of you. I know it's hard to be patient, but he will be with you soon."

The effect is immediate—her frown softens, her body relaxes. She nuzzles into his neck, completely placated. I've never seen her respond so quickly to anyone's reassurance, not even mine. He knew exactly what to say to her, right down to calling them idiots.

I turn back to Tim.

"Oh, and call her usual driver. Tell her she can go home; Evelyn won't need her."

"Anything else?"

"Yes, and—"

Finn's stomach growls again—a sound so at odds with his ethereal appearance that I almost laugh.

Evelyn sits up, suddenly all business.

"You're hungry," she says to Finn, as if this is a shocking revelation. Then she turns to the others, waving a dismissive hand. "You three may go. Get my Finny some food! But don't go far!" The authoritative CEO is back, albeit naked and covered in alpha bite marks. Chris, Preston, and Tim all straighten obediently at her command.

"We'll be right outside," Chris says, already moving toward the door.

Preston follows, shooting me a look that says, "Good luck," more clearly than words.

As they file out, I approach the nest. Before I lie down, I say, "Tim, the 'In-Office Heat Contingency Plans' tab has a pivot table. You can enter various criteria—"

She grabs me by the collar and yanks me into the nest with her, guiding me to lie beside her, opposite Finn.

"There," she sighs, sandwiched between us, sounding completely satisfied. "My boys."

CHAPTER 10

We file out of Evelyn's office, a somber procession of half-starved, lower-ranked pack members banished from the nest by our omega's command.

"And shut the door. The light is too bright!" Evelyn commands. The door clicks shut with quiet finality.

I've never felt more like an outsider in my life.

My shoulders hunch forward like I'm carrying the weight of that alpha bark on my back. It echoes in my ears—my own voice, transformed into something ugly and commanding.

I can't believe I barked at her...

Everything was just happening so fast, and I...

"Bob's desk," Tim says, pointing at the workspace in front of us. "We need to make those calls."

I nod, not trusting my voice. My throat still feels raw, like I swallowed broken glass. Using the alpha bark always leaves me feeling hollow afterward, but this time the emptiness has teeth. My bark came in late—like everything about me.

I couldn't use it to protect her twenty years ago, and I can't use it to protect her now.

Bob's desk is meticulous: organized with the precision of a man who has a plan for everything, even desk accessory placement. Sticky notes line the edge of his computer monitor, each one covered in his tight, efficient handwriting. All of them mention Evelyn.

Preston stumbles slightly, all the light dulled from his movie star. His hot chocolate scent smells off—rewarmed, burned.

"You okay?" I ask him, resisting the urge to lurch for him as if he were a fainting maiden—alphas generally don't appreciate that type of attention, but I'm ready to do it if necessary.

"Never better," Preston lies with a weak smile. "Maybe I am too old for this," he jokes weakly. "Can't keep up with a young alpha like you. Whenever my mom would harass me, saying I needed to get an omega before I was too old to keep up with a heat, I thought she was just trying to rush me. I didn't think it might actually be true." He sways.

"Sit down," I tell him, pulling the chair from the desk and offering it to him.

Preston sinks into the chair gratefully and nods. "It feels like Finn's bark pulled the last bit of my soul from my body. No wonder all those fans used to melt during his concerts."

Tim perches on the edge of the desk. "I've never felt anything like that before."

That was my fault.

I sigh and lean next to Tim on the desk, keeping my eye on Preston. "I'm sorry, guys. This is my fault. I shouldn't have barked at her. I can't believe I barked at her," I groan. My hands brace the desk. Tim's hand covers the one between us. "I've been called an idiot more times today than probably my entire life."

Tim's hand moves to my shoulder, and he gives me a reassuring smile. "Does it make you feel better to know that idiot might as well be a term of endearment for her? She uses much harsher words for those she actually thinks are stupid."

Preston chuckles and says under his breath, "God, I love that woman." He leans back in the chair and looks like a little of his energy is returning to him.

Tim continues, but there's no judgment in his voice, just tired amusement. "But yeah, that bark was definitely not the smartest move."

"I know," I mumble. "I just—was trying to protect her."

"From what?" Preston asks, "From the arms of her fated mate?" He runs a hand through his hair, mussing it further. "It was obvious the moment that door opened, those two were pre-bonded somehow. Maybe you don't want to admit it, but you weren't protecting her; you were protecting yourself."

The truth of it stings, needling its way through my nervous system and stopping my heart as adrenaline floods my receptors. Every cell in my body screams, "Fight or flight!"

"Deny it! Fight it!" But I can't.

I have no counter-argument, no defense.

"Then run from it! Flee! Don't think about it!" But I shouldn't.

I sit here with the weight of my actions. I let my body do its internal thrashing and flailing and try to understand why that statement makes my body react this way.

Because he's right.

I wasn't trying to stop her to protect her. I was trying to stop her because I was scared of losing her.

I didn't care about what she needed—what she wanted. Well, I did, but I cared more about what I needed in that moment.

I told myself it was for her, but really, I was doing what made me feel better. She was telling me what she wanted, but I didn't want to hear it. And I justified my actions to her and to myself by saying I was protecting her.

She opened the door, and instead of letting her do what she needed, I tried to pull her closer because I wanted her to comfort me more than I wanted to comfort her.

Preston kicks my foot, getting my attention, and says, "Hey. You'll feel better once you bond with her. You'll know how she feels without having to see through that angry, sexy armor of hers."

"Yeah. She'll still call you an idiot," Tim says, nudging my shoulder with his. "But maybe you'll stop acting like such an idiot."

I look at my feet. "There's no way she'll bond with me now. After what I did?" I swallow hard. "After...him?"

Finn, Zane, whatever he calls himself, why does she need another alpha if she has one like him?

Preston says, conviction in his voice. "She said she would. She said she was going to bond with all of us." But the conviction in his voice wavers—he's likely considering his own relationship with her.

"But what if she doesn't?" The question slips out before I can stop it, raw and vulnerable.

Neither responds.

Why would she want to bond with me? What do I have to offer?

Her thoughts haven't been consumed with the idea of me for the last twenty years. I'm just some guy who showed up and said, "Hey, remember that one thing I did twenty years ago? You should love me now because of it!"

You're nothing without her. Sure, you're big, but really, you're weak, powerless, pathetic. Protecting her will prove it. It will prove you are worthy of her love.

And suddenly…I get it.

The idea clicks into place like one of those old slides on a projector. The dial in my head turns, focusing on it.

I've held her in my head for so long. I've wrapped my whole identity around one thing: her. So when she didn't immediately act the exact way I wanted, I panicked. I wanted her to come to me, tell me how much she needed a big, strong alpha around. Tell me I was necessary. And when she didn't…I tried to control her.

When she opened that door, I saw the last hope of being the primary alpha, the position I needed to prove I was enough, fly away. So instead of trusting she'd come back, I had to hold her tight, make her do what I wanted. And what I wanted was for her to prove to me I was important enough to her that she'd never leave.

I can't control her.

I thought I wasn't trying to, but I was. I was trying to make her love me the way I wanted her to. To give me the security I need. But…what I need to do is be myself and trust that it is enough.

Because the only person I can control, or should control, is myself.

But I don't need to be first. I just need to be hers. I just need to be me.

I sigh. "Preston, you're right. I was trying to protect myself. I was so scared of being at the bottom of the hierarchy."

Tim snorts, a grin breaking across his face. "Well, you do make an excellent bottom."

Heat rises in my cheeks at the memory of bottoming for Tim earlier. "Jesus, Tim," I blush, my self-loathing now replaced with a mixture of pride, bashfulness, and—I can't believe I still have it in me right now—arousal.

I swoon.

Actually, that wasn't a swoon. That was a wobble—a near faint.

"I wish I had eaten more for lunch," I say, rubbing the back of my neck. "I knew salads wouldn't be enough." I groan. I have to figure out how to communicate with Evelyn without imposing my will on her or capitulating to her.

Tim looks at his phone. "Looks like the driver just picked up the food. Shouldn't be much longer."

I nod.

"Watch out, Preston. Let me get to Bob's computer," Tim says, rising from his perch and walking behind the desk. Preston rolls back.

Tim wiggles the mouse, and the screen blinks to life, revealing a lock screen. The way he leans over reminds me of us fucking, and I do my best to keep all the blood in my head because I might actually pass out if I let it go elsewhere.

"Shit, he didn't tell us his password, did he?" Tim says, straightening up, looking at the door.

None of us wants to go back in there right now. I don't even want to think about what she'd do if we returned without food for her, "Finny."

"Try 'Evelyn'," Preston suggests.

Tim types it in, and the screen flashes red. "Nope."

"'Evelyn1' then," Preston suggests, leaning forward.

Another try, another rejection.

"Maybe something to do with foxes and omegas? 'FoxyOmega'?" I suggest.

Tim tries it. No luck.

"Wait," Preston says, "Try 'Evelyn1', but put an exclamation point at the end."

Tim types. The screen unlocks, revealing Bob's desktop. The background is a group photo of all the company's employees. All the icons on the desktop are arranged so that the only face not covered is, you guessed it, Evelyn's. Bob is standing right next to her, and Tim is on the other side. There are hundreds of employees.

I say, "Wow, I didn't realize how big this company was."

Tim says, "Yeah, it takes a lot of people to make a game, and we always have multiple projects running. We have a lot of remote employees, too."

Preston leans forward, tapping the screen next to Tim, "What the heck is that?"

Tim chuckles, "Oh, that's Styles...well, her proxy. That's from a few years ago. It's much cooler now."

I peer down. It looked like a Mars rover with a screen on top. On the screen is a beautiful blonde omega woman who looks like she'd rather be anywhere but there... even though she isn't.

Preston laughs. "Styles is a character. Have you met her, Chris?"

I shake my head. "No, but Tim's told me about her."

Preston reflects. "I've only been on a few video calls with her, but... she's got this aura of genius about her. You can tell she's a million steps ahead of you. Like she already knows what you're going to say before you do and she's just waiting for your slow brain to catch the fuck up."

Tim laughs. "You have absolutely no idea how true that is." Less fascinated with the idea of Styles than Preston or I are, Tim returns to the task of finding the file Bob told us to look for.

The mess of folders is a bit overwhelming, and it takes us a while to find the folder we need. Everything is organized, but in a system only Bob knows. It's like a complex code whose cipher is 'Evelyn'.

Tim clicks on a folder labeled 'Evelyn's Heat'.

Inside are dozens of sub-folders, organized in the same indecipherable system I can't quite parse: 'Food Preferences', 'Nest Materials', 'Schedule', 'Mood Tracking', 'Medication', 'Previous Heat Data', etcetera.

"Jesus," I breathe, both impressed and slightly unnerved by the level of detail.

"Holy shit, this dude is devoted," Preston says, staring at the desktop.

Tim absentmindedly opens the 'Food Preferences' folder, revealing a spreadsheet that tracks not only Evelyn's favorite foods but when she prefers them during her heat cycle, cross-referenced with her mood and energy levels.

"I've known Bob for years," Tim says, scrolling through the document with growing amazement, "and I had no idea he was this... thorough."

Preston whistles low. "This isn't just devotion. This is worship. I mean...I get it. If my brain worked like this, I'd probably be doing the same."

Tim opens another folder labeled 'Schedule' and finds a color-coded calendar that plots out the next three weeks in painstaking detail. Each day of Evelyn's expected heat is broken down into two-hour blocks, with notes about expected intensity, preferred activities, and even which staff member from her support team is on call.

He closes the schedule. "Okay, so we're looking for something to do with contact information or contingency plans, right?"

"Yeah," I say, overwhelmed with how much stuff there is. "Fuck, maybe we should just go back in there and ask Bob."

We all look at the door and feel the waves of candy cane roiling out. *Prime Alpha.* Our attention returns to the computer—an unspoken fear and agreement between us.

"Look at this," Tim says, pointing to a file labeled 'Alpha Support'.

We glance at each other, feeling like we've found a secret we shouldn't look for—it might as well be labeled "Pandora's Box". Tim opens it, not needing Preston or me to egg him on. Within it, we see a long list of high-powered alphas, each with a headshot, detailed notes on their scents, compatibility with Evelyn, sexual preferences, the likelihood that Evelyn would want their assistance, etcetera.

Preston points at the first alpha on the list. "Come on, Bob!? This guy. He's a total douche!" Then he looks at me and asks, "You think we're listed in here?"

"I don't think I want to know," I grimace.

Tim closes the file before our curiosity continues to get the best of us. But, instead of resuming his search, he stares at the computer, dazed.

I place my hand on his shoulder. "Tim, you okay? Do you need to sit down?"

"No wonder she bonded with him first," Tim says, his voice soft. "He's been taking care of her like this for years."

There's a flicker of sadness in his eyes, the slight downturn of his mouth. "Does this make you feel better? Or worse?" I ask, unsure if I can read his emotions.

"I…I don't know," he admits. "I've known her longer. But I never…I never did this." He gestures at the screen, at the evidence of Bob's devotion.

I squeeze his shoulder gently.

Preston, who's been quietly scanning the screen, says, "What about that one, 'Contact Information'?"

Tim snaps out of his daze and clicks the folder. There's a spreadsheet with what appears to be the contact information for every person and business in the city.

"There," Preston says, pointing at a tab labeled 'In-Office Heat Contingency Plans'.

"Hell yeah," Tim says, and we all feel weirdly triumphant for finding the needle in the haystack.

Tim clicks on it, and the elation is replaced with a: "What the fuck, Bob? How am I supposed—" He doesn't even finish. Doesn't need to. The tab is organized by various contingency plans, which seem to be grouped by data points: number of alphas, time of year, severity of Evelyn's last heat, the company's current revenue stream, and whether the limited-edition milkshake she loves is offered at the local fast food joint.

Preston asks, "Was this dude like a spy or a data analyst or something in a past life?"

Tim's eyebrows furrow. "I think…I think he actually started in QA and then moved into this role. It was before I worked here."

Preston leans forward and puts his elbows on his knees, head hanging between his shoulders. "Damn, all this data is making me dizzy," he says, pressing a hand to his forehead. His pupils are dilated, his skin flushed, and his hot-chocolate scent smells like it was burnt then left out to spoil.

This seems like more than just hunger. He might be having adverse withdrawal effects.

I kneel in front of him, grab his face between my hands, and look into each of his eyes, wishing I had a flashlight. "Hey, Tim, gimme your phone." He does, and I shine the light into Preston's eyes. Instead of constricting as they should, his pupils dilate. Then I see the milky white haze of a beast pooling in his pupils.

Fuck.

I try not to sound concerned. "What brand patch were you using?"

Preston just shrugs. "I have no idea."

"Could you call your pharmacy and find out?"

Preston grimaces. "So...knowing my packmate Derek, it's not pharmaceutical."

I nod, understanding the biology at play. I turn off the flashlight and return Tim's phone to him. "You'll be okay, but we need to get you some food. Your body is burning through reserves fast and...you're going through suppressant withdrawal."

"What? What does that mean?"

"Mostly, that you won't be able to control your rut. But also that you need food," I tell him, "and water. Lots of both."

Preston's eyes glaze over, the rut fog setting in. "I just need to close my eyes for a minute," he murmurs, slumping lower in the chair.

"Not a great idea," I warn him. "Sleep now, and you'll wake up in full rut with no fuel in your system."

But he's already drifting, his body shutting down non-essential functions to conserve energy for when his mate calls him to her nest. His breathing deepens, and within seconds, he's asleep, head tilted back against the chair.

"Well, that's not ideal," Tim remarks.

"He'll be fine once we get some food in him," I say. "But, I'm going to have to monitor him for signs of cardiac arrest." I turn back to the computer. "We're going to need Bob for this, aren't we?"

"Yeah." Tim looks at his phone. "Food's here. Let's at least do that."

CHAPTER 11

BOB

SOS. All hands on deck. Chris can cum 2.

I show the text to Chris, who raises an eyebrow. "Nice to know I'm allowed," he says dryly.

"Hey," I reply, stepping out as the elevator doors open, food in hand. "Maybe it means she's not mad anymore."

I know that it just as likely means Evelyn's heat is overriding her anger and logic, but the guy needs all the pep talks I can give.

We run as quickly as we can back to the nest, overwhelmed by the sheer volume of food delivery bags we're trying to juggle. The closer we get, the stronger the scents become: gingerbread and candy cane dominant, with threads of cinnamon and hot chocolate weaving through.

"Shit, Preston is awake, rutting in there. He's going to fucking kill himself," Chris says, somehow running faster. I push open the door, and the scent hits me like a physical force, nearly buckling my knees.

The visual follows a half-second later: Evelyn on her hands and knees in the center of her nest, Preston behind her, his hips moving in the relentless rhythm of deep rut. He's not just having sex with her; he's rutting, fully lost to the primitive drive that can overtake an alpha. He looks like a different person; the smile that usually curves his lips is gone, and his eyes are milky white—the vestigial remnants of our shape-shifter ancestors clouding in his irises and screaming, "I was an evolutionary advantage, you fucks! Why'd you naturally select me out?"

At her head, Bob and Finn kneel on either side, both murmuring soft words I can't quite catch. Bob strokes her hair while Finn holds her face in his hands, thumbs gently caressing her cheeks. The gentleness of their touch contrasts sharply with the intensity of Preston's thrusts.

"Tim," Bob calls, looking up with relief. "Thank God. We need all the help we can get."

My body reacts. I'm already stepping forward, already unbuttoning my shirt, already rock hard just from the pheromones saturating the air.

Behind me, a loud crash turns my attention to Chris. The multitude of bags he was carrying are at his feet, their contents spilled across the floor. His chest is heaving, he stares forward with a look of confusion as exhaustion addles his brain, and he fights his urge to rut right next to Preston.

"Tim," Evelyn breathes, returning my attention to her. Evelyn's eyes find mine, and the recognition there makes my heart skip. Even in the throes of her heat, even with Preston's knot swelling inside her, she knows me. Sees me. Calls for me.

I cross to her quickly, shedding my remaining clothes as I go. I settle in beside Finn, who shifts to avoid contact with me without taking his hands from Evelyn's face.

Up close, the scent of her is even more intense—gingerbread and need and *mine*.

"I'm here," I tell her, cupping her cheek. "What do you need?"

Instead of answering, she surges forward, taking me into her mouth with such sudden hunger that I gasp, my knees weakening.

She moans around me, the vibration traveling up my spine like electricity. Her mouth is hot and wet, her rhythm matching Preston's thrusts from behind.

"She's been asking for you," Bob says softly, still stroking her hair. "Both of you."

I glance over at Chris, who stands frozen by the door, his

expression a complex mixture of desire and uncertainty. He always holds back, so scared of doing harm, he won't let his desires overtake him.

Evelyn pulls off me and whips her head toward him. "Hey, dick for brains," she calls, voice raspy and breathless, "be useful!"

Well, at least she didn't call you an idiot again, right?

The command breaks whatever spell was holding Chris in place. He moves forward, unbuttoning his shirt, his green eyes darkening with want. He approaches the nest cautiously, like he's not sure where he fits. He watches Finn, waiting to see if he will bark him out the nest, but Finn's eyes, as they have been since they first found Evelyn, are locked on her.

"Here," Bob says, shifting to make room. "Take over for me."

Chris hesitates only a moment before kneeling where Bob indicates, his hands immediately finding Evelyn's shoulders. She leans into his touch with a satisfied sigh, then returns her attention to me, taking me deep again, her tongue doing things that make coherent thought impossible.

Preston's rhythm falters, his breathing growing ragged. He grits his teeth, tightens his grip on Evelyn's hips, and lets out a primal howl.

She whimpers around me, the sound somewhere between pleasure and demand. Finn leans down, whispers something in her ear that makes her whole body shudder.

"Yes," she gasps, pulling off me again. "All of you. I need all of you."

And then, we move. Working as a team to make sure we give our omega exactly what she needs. Bob repositions to help support her weight. Chris remains at her head, occasionally stealing kisses from her lips between her attentions to me. Finn's hands explore Evelyn's body with reverent touches.

The scent of hot chocolate and gingerbread spikes, triggering a response of snow and pine from Chris and candy cane from Finn. Bob and I also respond, unthinkingly releasing cinnamon and spiced cranberries into the air.

A Christmas feast just for her: the woman who hates Christmas.

Chris and Finn's eyes dilate and cloud white, too, but not as drastically as Preston's. Their already opposing forms grow as their muscles contract, bulking their mass as if someone has a tire pump, steadily filling them.

I should be afraid—three alphas rutting, all with a claim on the omega whose mouth is wrapped around my cock—but instead, I feel a strange calm.

We're a pack now.

The instinctual drive that normally sets alpha against alpha—alpha against the world—presents not as aggression or possessiveness, but as care. All of them are focused on Evelyn's pleasure rather than their own dominance.

Preston's knot catches, locks, and he groans—a deep, animal sound that seems to vibrate through all of us. Evelyn comes undone beneath Preston's final thrusts, her body quaking, her mouth tightening around me in a way that nearly sends me over the edge.

Preston collapses against her back, locked inside her, his breath coming in harsh pants.

"Switch," Bob commands, his voice gentle but unmistakably authoritative. "She needs more."

What follows is a choreography of bodies, limbs, and desires that shouldn't work but somehow does.

Preston stays locked to Evelyn while the rest of us rearrange.

Chris moves behind her, his hands taking over from Preston's, supporting her through the aftershocks. I find myself face to face with her again, but this time it's Bob who guides my cock back to her mouth, his own hand wrapped around the base.

"Open up, baby," Bob says, his voice a low rumble. "The cock you were begging for."

Evelyn hums in happiness, the vibration sending pleasure shooting up my spine.

Bob shifts to Evelyn's side, running a cool cloth over her heated skin, occasionally offering sips of water when she pauses for breath.

Preston's knot recedes, and as he carefully separates from Evelyn, Chris is there immediately, his hands steadying her. She turns toward him, surprising us all by capturing his mouth in a fierce kiss.

"Fuck you," she murmurs against his lips, "now fuck me."

Chris nods, solemn and sincere. "I'm sorry."

"Show me," she challenges, and then they're moving together, Chris lifting her effortlessly as she guides him inside her.

The rest of us shift to accommodate this new configuration, creating a cocoon of bodies around them.

Time loses meaning as we cycle through various combinations—Evelyn with Chris, then with Finn again, then with Preston.

Sometimes two of us at once, sometimes taking turns.

Nothing seems to break her lust: not orgasm, not knot, not us...

My vision blurs as I pull out of Evelyn and spill across the small of her back, pleasure ripping through me like a lightning strike, taking my last reserve of energy.

My legs shake, knees threatening to buckle as wave after wave crashes through my body. I gasp her name, one hand still gripping her hip, the other braced against a pile of cushions to keep from collapsing. But even as my own release overtakes me, I don't feel pleasure; all I feel is defeat.

We can't do this. I can't do this.

We're not enough. I'm not enough.

We've been at it for God knows how long, but it hasn't been enough. Evelyn's heat demands more from us. Her body is desperately chasing a release she can't catch. Every orgasm she's had feels like a lotto draw, each of us anxiously holding our breath, wondering, "Is that the winning ticket?"

Her mind is lost to the drive of her heat. All recognition in her eyes is gone, and she looks at us as if we're sex toys whose batteries have died and warranties have expired.

Chris is beneath Evelyn, on his back, eyes closed, as she rides his knot, her movements frantic and unsatisfied.

His hands span her waist, guiding her, his brow furrowed in concentration despite the exhaustion etched in every line of his face.

"That's it, sweetheart," he murmurs, voice cracking with fatigue. "You're so close."

But she's not.

Finn kneels before her, his white-blond hair darkened with sweat at the temples, his cock disappearing between her lips as she sucks aggressively. He sings, "Babygirl, your fever is back. And if I'm not enough, we'll form a pack. Omegababy." The words catch in his throat, exhausted from so much use after so much silence.

Preston is sprawled on the floor next to the nest. He rutted himself unconscious, his body finally giving out after hours of exertion and hunger. He looks half-dead, all color drained from his flesh, and his normally perfect hair is plastered to his forehead. He looks like he needs a doctor, but the doctor on duty is currently holding on to what may be our last hope of breaking this Omega's heat flare.

Holding the finally recharged knot vibrator like an exhausted knight holding a sword right before the dragon douses him in flames, Bob moves immediately to take my place behind Evelyn. He slides it into her, working her ass with gentle determination while his other hand finds her clit, rubbing in small, precise circles of a man whose hand is locked in the pains of carpal tunnel syndrome but is pushing through it.

"Come on, baby," he whispers, voice hoarse from hours of similar encouragements. "Let go for us. We've got you."

But we don't. We don't got shit.

We're losing this battle.

I stumble backward, my legs finally giving out. My body feels hollow, emptied.

Another casualty of war.

Evelyn whimpers, the sound shooting straight through me like a physical pain. She rocks desperately between Chris's knot, Finn's cock, and Bob's vibrator, seeking something that hovers just beyond her reach. Her skin is flushed deep red, her hair a wild tangle clinging to her sweat-slick shoulders. She looks feral, desperate, caught in the grip of a heat that seems determined to break her.

"I'm sorry, sweetheart, we're trying," Chris says, his voice barely audible. The words carry the weight of failure, of inadequacy. He can't make her come right now.

None of us can.

Chris winces. "I don't have much left in me."

I try to get it up. But I can't. My dick lies against my leg, flaccid, pathetic, just like everything else about me.

"I don't know how she planned on doing this alone," Bob says, his fingers never stopping their careful ministrations. "I have a roster of alphas we could call in for help. Tim, do you have enough energy to take over for me so I can make some calls?"

The words hit me like a physical blow. A sob catches in my throat, raw and ugly.

Seeing the roster earlier started a slow drip of despair in the sediments of my confidence and has been slowly corroding away the bedrock of my heart. Those words are the final drop, opening up the massive sinkhole of misery within me.

Perfect, prepared Bob, who thinks of everything, who has contingencies for contingencies. Bob, with whom Evelyn bonded first. Bob, who's been by her side for years, anticipating her needs before she even knows them herself. Bob had created a list of alphas to help her because he knew I would never be able to.

Something breaks inside me—a dam holding back emotions I've been too exhausted to process. Tears spill out, sudden and unstoppable, down my cheeks before I can think to hide them.

"You think of everything. I guess that's why she bonded with you, not me, Bob," I choke out, the words tearing from somewhere deep and wounded.

I'll never be enough.

I'm not an alpha.

I'm not even a good beta.

The room goes still. Even Evelyn pauses, Finn's cock slipping from her mouth as she turns her head toward me.

But I can't stop now. The words keep coming, dragged up from a place I've kept carefully hidden for years. "You're so fucking perfect for her. Always prepared. Always know exactly what she needs. And what am I? Just...just the guy who happened to be there for her first heat. The one who played your songs on repeat while she suffered," I say, nodding toward Finn without looking at him. "Because I wasn't enough then. Just like I'm not enough now. I'm never enough. I'm not an alpha. I'm a shit beta."

I turn to Chris. "I could have been the biggest guy, but you fucking beat me to that. Or I could have been the jokester, but Sleeping Beauty beat me on that." I thumb toward Preston. "I'm fucking nothing. I'm just Tiny Tim, the boy who cries after he shoots his load on your ass."

I drag a blanket across my face, trying to stem the tears that won't stop flowing. "I don't have a roster of backup alphas. I don't have a medical degree. I don't have a Hollywood career or platinum records or a beautiful smile or a dick the size of her forearm. I'm just...Tim. Just stupid, ordinary Tim who's loved her since we were kids and never had the guts to tell her. Why am I even here? To take up space? To take up resources? She doesn't need me. I can't even comfort her. She comforts me all the time. I should just leave."

Evelyn makes a sound—not a whimper this time, but something deeper, more protective. I look up to see her eyes locked on mine, pupils blown wide, nostrils flaring as she scents my distress. She shifts, trying to move toward me, but Chris's knot holds her in place.

I continue my tirade of tragedy, "See! Even in her heat haze, she's trying to protect and comfort me!"

"Evie, wait," Chris says, trying to steady her. "You'll hurt yourself."

She ignores him, struggling against the bond of their joined bodies, her gaze never leaving my face. A growl tears from her throat, the sound so unlike her that it freezes us all.

"Mine," she hisses, the word barely recognizable through the fierce snarl of her teeth.

"Evelyn," Bob says, his hands falling away from her body as he recognizes what's happening. "Chris, you need to turn. Let her reach him."

Chris nods and shifts onto his side, still locked inside Evelyn, maneuvering so that she's facing me. The position must be uncomfortable for him, but he doesn't complain. Finn backs away, giving her space, humming now instead of singing.

Evelyn reaches for me, her fingers clawing at the air between us. I move forward automatically, drawn by the desperation in her eyes, my own pain momentarily forgotten in the face of her need.

"Tim," she says, my name a broken sound on her lips. "Tim. Tim. Tim."

I take her outstretched hand, and she pulls with surprising strength, dragging me closer until I'm kneeling right in front of her. Her free hand fists in my hair, yanking my head to the side to expose my neck.

"Mine!" she shouts.

This is what's supposed to happen.

"Yours," I whisper, the word more breath than sound. "I've always been yours, Evie."

Her eyes soften for just a moment, a flash of the Evelyn I know shining through the heat-driven frenzy. Then her lips pull back in a snarl, and she lunges forward, teeth sinking into the junction of my neck and shoulder.

Pain explodes outward from the point of contact, sharp and electric. I cry out, my body jerking in response. But beneath the pain, there's something else—a current of connection, of rightness, threads of fate sewing us all together.

The sensation spreads through me, warming as it goes, transforming from pain to something deeper, more profound.

My body, my everything, is one with her.

"MINE!" Evelyn screams against my skin, her teeth still locked in my flesh. Her body convulses, back arching impossibly as the orgasm finally breaks through her. I feel it as if it's happening to me—waves of pleasure so intense they border on pain, crashing through her body and into mine through the newly formed bond.

Chris groans, his arms tightening around her waist as her internal muscles clamp down on his knot. Finn's eyes widen, feeling the link passing through us. Bob makes a soft sound of wonder, his hand coming to rest on the small of Evelyn's back, as he feels it, too.

Nothing else matters. Nothing. Except this: Evelyn's teeth in my neck.

Evelyn's climax seems endless, her cries muffle against my skin as she rides out wave after wave. When she finally releases my neck, she slumps forward, her forehead resting against my collarbone, her breath coming in ragged pants.

"Tim," she whispers, her voice wrecked but somehow tender. "My Tim."

I curl my arms around her, cradling her against me as best I can with

Chris still locked inside her. "I'm here," I promise, pressing my lips to her sweat-damp hair. "I'm not going anywhere."

She lifts her head, her eyes meeting mine. The feral wildness has receded, replaced by a clear, steady gaze that sees right through me. "You're not nothing," she says, each word deliberate despite her exhaustion. "You're mine. Always have been."

The last of my tears spills over. "Always will be," I tell her.

CHAPTER 12

I watch Evelyn, my love, my life, my everything, breathe. Every rise and fall of her chest feels like a minor miracle I've been granted permission to witness.

She finally rests—my sweet omegababy.

My fingers trace the waves of her brown locks, still damp with sweat from her heat. She smells like gingerbread and home—a home I've never had but recognize in my bones. My other hand covers my mouth, my mask long ago lost.

Her face in sleep lacks the sharp edges she wears awake. The furrow between her brows has smoothed, and her perpetually downturned mouth rests in neutrality.

This is the Evelyn I've always seen beneath the armor she dons to protect herself from the harshness of others.

My Evelyn.

My omegababy.

The most recent wave of heat was particularly difficult. For a moment, I thought she might kill us all—fully drain our life force just to fulfill her need.

I'd welcome it.

Anything for her.

Like characters in one of her video games, we were a guild of under-leveled, under-prepared warriors, failing endlessly against the final boss that severely outranked us.

I'd expect nothing less from her.

I sit on the edge of my beautiful ice dragon's nest, careful to avoid the touch of anyone but her.

Chris lies on her other side with Tim, their steady breaths warming her shoulder. Preston is curled at her feet like a watchful guardian. Bob occupies the space near her head, his fingers occasionally brushing against mine as we both pet her hair. I pull back. They can touch her—they must, for her comfort—but I don't need to touch them.

Arranged like dying planets orbiting a sun, we lie here spent, recovering energy as we await the next solar flare.

Well, not all of us.

Bob, the one who has always taken care of my love, kisses her atop the head, then carefully extricates himself from the nest, movements precise and gentle to avoid disturbing Evelyn. The loss of his body heat creates a small void that the others unconsciously shift to fill, moving closer to her.

I remain still, maintaining my vigil, my fingers never ceasing their gentle caress of her hair, my eyes never leaving her perfect face.

"Where are you going?" Tim asks, his voice barely audible.

"Food. Electronics," Bob whispers back. "We'll need them. We won't have much time before she wakes back up, and I'll need all of your assistance."

Tim shifts in the nest, his arm draped protectively over Evelyn's waist, his arm careful not to disturb her as he adjusts position. "She seems comfortable. How long do you think she'll sleep?" he whispers.

Chris responds, pressing his hand to her forehead and checking his watch. "Maybe a few hours. I wish I had a thermometer. If I could track her temperature, I could predict it. Based on the timing of her waves, we haven't even hit the worst of it yet."

So it wasn't even my boss baby's final form? That's what I get for underestimating her.

I stare down at her, marveling at her power and beauty.

Out of the corner of my eye, Bob moves efficiently around the office. First, he gathers the food and water that haven't been scavenged over the last few hours and gives them to Chris to dispense. Then he sorts the strewn clothing, retrieving things from pockets.

My eyes remain on my Evelyn.

"Finn," someone says—Chris, I think, but I don't care. "Food?"

I don't look up.

Styrofoam packaging appears on my lap. I don't look up, but I do remove my hand from my face to open the packaging. I need energy for my love. I will not let her down in her time of need. I eat the meal, without much acknowledgement of its contents. The only senses I care to perceive are the ones that perceive Evelyn.

Chris clears his throat. "So, Finn," he tries, leaning forward slightly. "You've known our Evelyn for a while, I gather?"

Silence.

"It's like we're not even here," Chris mutters to someone, likely me, but I don't care.

Exactly. I'd prefer you weren't here.

"You doing okay over there, Finn?" Tim's voice is soft, careful not to wake Evelyn.

I stroke a strand of hair from her forehead and say nothing.

"I think that's a 'yes,'" Preston murmurs with a laugh. "I've known Finn for a while now. He doesn't talk."

Chris says, "But, he's been speaking this whole time."

Not to you.

Preston mumbles as if there is food in his mouth, "Yeah, well, I guess he talks to her."

Exactly. Her. Not you. Stop trying.

Chris tries again. "So, he's Zayn from Fates Five? The pop star who disappeared twenty years ago." I offer no response.

Preston sighs. "I guess so. I had no idea. Never seen him until today." He makes a noise as if he's eating. Then continues, "I've always known him as DJ THNTS.exe," mispronouncing the name the way everyone does. "But, just back off. He's not a fan of proximity. Don't touch him or look him in the eye. He doesn't like that."

Chris asks, "Like, he's going to bark at us if we dare touch him?"

Preston replies, "No, like, he's got social anxiety, don't touch him. Just stop crowding him."

The weight of the nest shifts, as Chris relents.

Thanks, Preston.

I've always liked Preston. He's never challenged or questioned my proclivities; he's just accepted them and ensured his team followed my wishes. I accept the fact that my love needs other alphas; her deiform insatiability obviously too much for the measly strength of a pathetic mortal such as myself. But accepting something and being happy about it are two different matters. However, I suppose if she has to have other alphas worshipping her, I am happy Preston is one of her devotees.

I finish my food, put the container to the side, careful not to soil my love's nest, and return my full attention to her. My other hand drifts back to cover my face.

The nest rustles as Bob slides back into position, careful not to disturb the sleeping beauty. He places her phone within easy reach in front of her face. She'll wake and immediately look for it, and he's prepared for that inevitability. Then he puts my phone at my side, with my mask on top. He doesn't bother trying to distract me from my love; he simply places it at my side.

I've always found Bob's attention to detail striking. He anticipates her needs before she ever speaks them. I like him for that. But it seems he anticipates not just her needs. Bob is another whom I accept, albeit reluctantly, as a fellow congregant at The Church of Evelyn.

I put on my mask. Its return to my mouth is so welcome, you would think it was my love's gentle folds I was nestling my mouth within, not a simple medical mask. With it, I am more comfortable looking at the others as they move around the nest.

Bob begins muttering to himself. "...if the snow picks up...and it takes 45 minutes on...what about? No...okay...yeah...and then we can... alright..." I glance in his direction, curious about what he's working on for the sake of my omegababy. He's tapping his tablet, sorting through a spreadsheet, as the screen's lights illuminate his face in a way that amplifies his concern.

Preston props himself up on one elbow. "Bob, what's the plan? We can't stay here for another wave like that one."

Bob just holds up a finger, and we all remain silent, allowing him to maintain his focus. Well, his focus isn't why I remain silent, but I remain silent nonetheless.

After a few moments, Bob looks at the rest of us, his plan worked out in his head. "Time for Contingency Plan A5," Bob says with confidence generally uncharacteristic of a beta. "We're going to have to hustle, but I think we can have everything ready before she wakes. I should be able to get everything here within an hour. Hopefully, she'll be asleep for the next few hours. If she wakes before then, we can implement Contingency Plan A7."

Here I was thinking I was Evelyn's most devoted follower. But, it seems I was mistaken. Bob has been sitting in her pews, silently worshipping her, for years.

"You really thought of everything," Tim says, echoing my thoughts.

Bob shrugs, uncomfortable with the praise. "It's my job."

It's not, actually.

"It's more than a job to you," Preston observes.

My fingers continue their gentle rhythm through Evelyn's hair as I silently agree. Bob's dedication goes beyond professional obligation.

Evelyn stirs slightly under my touch, her face turning toward my hand. Even in sleep, she seeks comfort from her alphas. From me. The trust in this unconscious gesture makes my chest tight with an unfamiliar warmth.

Bob continues working on his tablet, implementing this supposed Contingency Plan A5, as the others chat amongst themselves, becoming familiar with their new packmates. They've stopped asking me questions, which I appreciate. Still, I do find myself listening to their conversation with slightly above apathetic attention; however, whenever the topic turns to Evelyn, which it often does, my attention peaks.

Preston has been shoveling food into his mouth, determined not to pass out again, and making jokes about how surprised he is that alphas trying to shed weight for movie roles don't enlist omegas in heat rather than personal trainers. Now he lies content and full on Evelyn's opposite side. "So, Bob. You said earlier that Evelyn stopped taking her suppressants? Why'd she quit?"

Bob's fingers stop their rhythmic tablet tapping. His scent shifts subtly, laced with a bitterness that makes my heart ache. Mine does the same, because I, too, know the answer to the question—I was there, witnessing the devastation that led to her decision in real time. The others look at me, reading my emotions on my scent.

"Her pack left her," Bob finally says, the words clipped and hard. "About three weeks ago. They got in her head about her suppressants, being an omega, all that."

The nest goes still with a collective intake of breath, and one after the other, cinnamon and candy cane are not alone in their anger.

That knowledge acts as a solvent, stripping away Preston's happy-go-lucky veneer. He growls, "What happened? She said she didn't want to go home because of them."

They were assholes. Fucking assholes.

"Assholes," Bob says with an edge in his voice. "Three alphas who didn't deserve to breathe the same air as her."

Yeah!

Tim's usually meek and anxious voice carries a bite to it when he says, "They'd been together for a few years. I don't recall how long. But...sometime after I started working here, right Bob?"

"Yeah, four years," Bob says, anger tinting his voice. "Jacob was the Prime Alpha. The other two were already packed with him when he met Evelyn." He pauses, closing his eyes as if centering himself. "They met at some conference. At first, it seemed like they liked how strong-willed she was. Like they saw it as a reflection of their own power, maybe?"

"Until they saw it as a reflection of their weakness," Preston guesses, his voice soft but dangerous.

"Yeah, I think so," Bob confirms. "I don't fully understand it. She didn't open up to me about most of it. But I'd hear little things in her conversations with Styles, with Tim, and I saw how she changed..."

"They were never good to her," Tim adds, his voice dropping even lower. "At first, it was subtle. Small comments about her work hours, her dedication to the company. They'd tell her if she really cared about the harmony of the pack, she'd stop taking suppressants. 'What kind of omega won't let her alphas mate mark her?' 'Your true purpose is to carry pups, not carry a company.' Stuff like that."

I stroke Evelyn's cheek with my knuckle, as gently as I can manage despite the rage coiling inside me.

Tim says, "By the end, they were really controlling. It got to a point where they wouldn't let me anywhere near her. I only ever saw her at work."

Bob adds, his voice cracking, "Toward the end, they were constantly fighting her about her suppressant usage. They were obsessed with it. Telling her she only made so much money to make them look bad. She never told me this, but...I'm pretty sure they barked at her—a lot. I could see it in the way her energy was drained out of her. She hasn't said it explicitly, but...I think she wanted to prove she could get through a heat without an alpha."

I close my eyes briefly, memories washing over me:

Standing in corners—unnoticed.
Watching. Helpless. Useless.
Purring—unheard.
Jacob's hand grips her arm too tightly.
Singing—unheard.
Mark rolls his eyes behind her back.
Lee barking at her.
Crying with her—unheard.
Evelyn purring herself to sleep alone.
Reaching out—unfelt.

If I had known it was real. If I hadn't convinced myself that it was psychosis, I could have...

"So she left them?" Chris asks, his scent sharpening with anger.

Tim shakes his head. "No, they left her. I guess those assholes finally accepted she wasn't going to let them mark her or knock her up. So, they gave up, told her she was 'too successful.' That her achievements made them feel 'emasculated.' That they needed an omega who would 'prioritize their needs over her career.'"

Preston's eyes narrow to dangerous slits. "They...said that? And they just walked out?"

"Worse. Left her a fucking note," Bob spits out, then immediately lowers his voice, glancing at Evelyn. She doesn't stir. "A note, after all those years. Said her, 'priorities weren't aligned with the pack's future.' That she'd, 'chosen her career over pack harmony.'" The semi-familiar phrasing makes the anger pang more poignantly.

"All of them left?" Chris asks, in disbelief. "At once?"

Bob nods, his eyes fixed on Evelyn's sleeping face. "Yeah. They were already a bonded trio before they added Evelyn. The other two followed him without hesitation."

"Fucking alphaholes," Preston finishes, his elegant fingers now curled into fists.

Bob nods. "Yeah."

"I could probably have them murdered," Preston says conversationally, so breezy. His tone is light, his eyes are warm, and it's a truly award-winning performance. But his scent, hot chocolate roiling on the pot, says he's a predator that shouldn't let his sweetness fool you; he can boil the flesh right off you, then coat you in chocolate and store you on a shelf as a trophy.

Chris's scent spikes with aggression, a snowstorm ripping through a forest, uprooting pines and impaling assholes with them. "I'd rather do it with my own hands," he says, his usual calm completely evaporated, not having the acting skills of Preston. "More satisfying. I'm a whiz with a scalpel. I can make it slow...painful."

My gaze shifts between them, something unfamiliar and warm uncoiling in my chest. These men—strangers until today—share my rage, my protective instinct toward Evelyn. It's disorienting and somehow comforting at the same time.

My pack. I forgot what this felt like.

I want to rip out her ex-pack's eyeballs, store them in jars, so they can watch how perfect she is every time I fuck her. Every time we fuck her. Maybe Preston and Chris can assist me with that. Preston can lure them in, Chris can remove the eyes...

Preston turns to Bob, his voice deliberately casual in a way that doesn't match the intensity of his scent. "So, Bob, hypothetically speaking, what are these gentlemen's full names, current addresses, and —for completely innocent reasons—social security numbers?"

The corner of Bob's mouth twitches, caught between amusement and his better nature. "I obviously can't tell you that," he says with visible reluctance, "even though I want to really badly." *I like Bob. This beta's got a little bite in him when it comes to our omega.*

I pull out my phone, the decision made before I've fully processed it. My thumbs move quickly over the screen, accessing information no one knows I possess and send Preston the following text message:

Jacob Eben - CEO Cornhill Games

Mark Ezers - CTO Cornhill Games

Lee Rogers - CFO Cornhill Games

The chime of Preston's phone cuts through the quiet room. When he reads the message, his disbelief mars his face. "How the hell do you know this?"

I can't exactly explain it, so I just type back:

Evelyn told me.

It's not a lie. It's just not the full truth.

My attention returns to Evelyn, my fingers resuming their gentle caress of her hair as if the exchange never happened.

Preston's confusion hangs in the air for a moment before he turns his phone toward Chris, showing him my text. Preston leans back slightly, his expression softening to contentment. "Well, this certainly simplifies things."

I look up from Evelyn for a moment, allowing myself to watch their reactions. The corner of my mouth curls into a small, wicked smile that I'm sure they can see under the mask. Preston returns it immediately, his grin equally predatory. Chris's smile is slower but equally dangerous, the healer showing the warrior beneath.

"Please don't kill them, you guys," Tim interjects with a sigh, breaking the moment. He glances between us, reading our expressions with growing concern.

Preston chuckles, the sound low and not entirely reassuring, no longer concerned with acting the part now that he has what he wants. "Of course, Tim. We're just joking...obviously...."

Chris nods solemnly. "Obviously."

Bob says, "Don't worry, Tim. When her heat passes, and they're done rutting, they'll stop thinking of murder."

Shows what he knows.

CHAPTER 13
Evelyn

For the first time today, I awake not with a jolt but with a slow, casual sleepiness. I surface gently, as if floating up from the depths of a warm sea.

It takes me a moment to realize I'm awake, as I register the darkness. There's something soft and heavy on my eyes, shielding the world from me—a weighted eye mask. My bare skin presses against something solid and warm. I can't see, but I know it's Finn. I pull down the mask to peer into his face and admire the unfamiliar angle of shadows that fall on his features and the ceiling above him.

"You're awake." Finn's voice rumbles through me, his chest vibrating against my spine. "How are you feeling?"

I reach up to stroke his beautiful face—pale, feminine and masculine at the same time—what I'd imagine an angel looks like. He nuzzles into my hand, purring, soothing me, kissing my palm.

Now that I've confirmed he's actually real, I say, "I'm...okay. Still tired." My voice comes out raspy, throat dry.

"You can rest, my love," he says, petting me and not breaking his gaze from me.

I try to sit up, but Finn's embrace tightens slightly. "Let me just hold you a moment longer, please. I'm not ready to share you yet."

Aww. Okay, my beautiful alphababy.

I turn my head, still in his lap, so I can peer out of my nest, and for a moment, I think that I'm not in my office. It has transformed into some sort of...well, I'm not entirely sure what. My mind struggles to process what I'm seeing.

"What the hell is going on?" I whisper to Finn.

Finn's chest rumbles against my back. "We're taking care of you."

The lights have been dimmed, colored, and changed to create a pleasing ambiance. And my furniture has been moved. It looks like... a spa.

The men—*my men?*—move with quiet purpose around the space, each focusing on a different task, all clad in matching robes in various colors–plush, fluffy things. The material is so soft-looking that my fingers itch to touch it.

I want to rub it on my face and probably my pussy.

Finn's arm appears, clad in a black version of the same material, in front of my face, as if reading my mind. I pull it to my face and snuggle it before returning my attention to the others.

Preston kneels beside a giant inflatable tub taking up the center of my office. He's got the sleeves of his robe rolled up like the good little slut he is, mixing various oils and bubbles into the tub. A hose snakes through the partially opened office door, filling the tub with water.

My desk has been pushed to a different corner of the room, which I'm really into; I might keep it there. Against the wall where my desk usually resides is a long table that looks like something you'd find at a buffet restaurant. It's covered with food warmers and chillers. I can't see what is inside the covered trays, but the smell makes my mouth water. And, holy fucking shit, right next to it is what looks like the soft serve machine from the fast food restaurant with my favorite milkshakes!

In the corner opposite my nest, Tim sits cross-legged on the floor. He appears to be making a second nest around a small television and retro video game consoles. He's arranged pillows and blankets in a perfect circle and topped it with so many adorable fox plushies my eyes water.

The rest of the room is arranged to maximize comfort. Fans are positioned evenly around the space, circulating the air and making everything feel less stale, less oppressive.

My eyes burn with unexpected tears. The care in every detail is overwhelming.

Chris enters through the doorway, muscles straining under the weight of what appears to be a small refrigerator. The door is only open for a second, but I catch a glimpse of crate after crate of supplies, as well as a table with rows upon rows of sex toys. They're arranged like weapons on a rack in an RPG fantasy game. As if the nest is a coliseum and these rut warriors can run out there and change out their weapons as they fight their opponent.

I return my attention to Chris. The veins in his forearms stand out, and I find myself staring, noticing how his biceps flex beneath his deep blue robe. *Ooo, another forearm slut. Momma likes.*

"Where do you want the cooling unit?" Chris asks Bob, straightening and rolling his shoulders.

"Next to the milkshake machine," Bob replies without looking up from his tablet.

Chris sets it down where Bob indicated, plugs it in, then returns to Bob's side to look at the tablet with him.

Chris points at the tablet. "We'll need to monitor her hydration levels and temperature carefully. We should also have ice packs rotating every four hours," Chris says, finger tracing something on Bob's tablet.

"Already taken care of," Bob responds, showing Chris something on the tablet. "I've scheduled alerts for hydration and temperature checks."

Chris says, "Now, I know we're all going to be tempted just to let her drink milkshakes and eat comfort foods all week, but we need to ensure she's getting appropriate nutrients. When possible, we should encourage natural, whole foods. The supplements should help reduce cramping and gland clotting during the murderous milkshake phase you warned us about. Did you order the supplements I suggested for her and the rest of us?"

Bob replies, "Yep, I've adjusted the meal deliveries scheduled for the next five days to include the anti-inflammatory menu, as you suggested, while also including the comfort foods. I also ordered the supplements you recommended, tailored to each of our individual needs."

Chris looks pensively at the ceiling, "We'll need to make sure we're keeping a tidy place. There are enough of us in the nest without introducing a team of bacteria. She'll fight us on it, though, wanting to remain in our scent, so let's order those diffusers you can mark."

Bob nods, his face serious in a way I rarely see outside of budget meetings. "I've arranged for fresh bedding delivery every six hours. The building has shut the shared HVAC off for the rest of the building. When other floors return after the holiday, they shouldn't be able to smell..."

"Good thinking," Chris murmurs, adding something to the list. "Oh, did you order—"

Something warm blooms in my chest as I watch them all.

"Finn," I whisper, sitting up to be in his lap and trying to keep my voice steady, "what is all this?"

He shifts behind me, tucking my head under his chin. "This, my love, is what Bob calls 'Contingency Plan A5.' He's had it ready for months, apparently. It just took a few calls to get in motion."

"Wha—why?"

"We were going to take you to your nest, but once you said you didn't want to, he pivoted."

"Bob did all this? For me?"

"Not just him," Finn confirms. "Tim insisted on the gaming station. He said that even when you're in your heat delirium, you'll still probably kick our asses at some old fighting game."

"Yeah, because I will," I laugh.

"I have no doubt, my love. He said it helps you manage your stress and winning while fucking actually makes you come harder."

I blush, but also mentally prepare to kick all these dude's asses. *Come at me, bros!*

Finn continues, "Chris has been adding medical supplies. Preston has been on the phone with one of his platonic packmates, asking for advice on how to create the perfect 'vibe.' He's been mixing that tub and arranging the furniture for a while now. And me...I knew if you didn't wake wrapped in someone's arms, you'd panic. So I waited."

I look around again, reassessing everything with this new

information. The careful preparation. The thoughtful touches. The way I woke without panic for the first time in…forever.

Each of them contributed something to help make sure I could weather my heat not just safely but…comfortably. They're creating a sanctuary for me, anticipating needs I didn't even know I had.

Something breaks inside me, a dam I didn't know was holding back an ocean.

Tears spill hot down my cheeks before I can stop them, my chest heaving with sobs that feel torn from somewhere deep and vulnerable.

The reaction is immediate.

All movement in the room stops. Four heads snap toward me, four sets of eyes widen in alarm. And then they're all moving at once, abandoning their tasks to circle me.

"Boss?" Bob is the first to speak, dropping to his knees beside where Finn holds me. "What's wrong? Are you in pain?"

Tim hovers anxiously, hands fluttering like he wants to touch me but isn't sure if he should. "Evie? Did we do something wrong? We can change anything."

Preston kneels beside me, looking at me with big Hollywood puppy eyes. "We're here for you, babygirl."

Chris discreetly grabs a thermometer and a cooling pack on his way toward me, hiding them in his pocket. "Are you feeling okay? Is your fever spiking? Is it cramping? Nausea?"

Finn just holds me tighter, his lips pressing against my hair.

I shake my head, unable to form words around the lump in my throat. How can I explain that no one has ever taken care of me like this? That I've spent so long trying to be strong and independent that I've forgotten what it feels like to be treasured?

"I just—" I hiccup, "I've never—" Another sob escapes.

Instead, I reach for them, one hand clutching Bob's sleeve, the other finding Tim's wrist. Finn holds me steady as Preston gently dabs at my tears, and Chris's warm palm comes to rest on my bare shoulder.

Five men. My five men. And for the first time in my life, I don't feel weak for needing them. I don't feel like it's going to come back to haunt me.

CHAPTER 14
Evelyn

"Tub's ready, babygirl," Preston announces, wiping his hands on a towel tucked into the belt of his robe. He looks pleased with himself, like an artist who's just finished a masterpiece.

But I don't want to bathe! I don't want to wash their scent off me.

Wait a minute! Why do they all smell wrong?

I whimper.

Finn says, "Don't worry, my love, you can mark them with your scent again soon."

I look at him, confused.

How does he keep reading my mind?

"Bond link, remember?" he says, with a smirk.

I grab at my neck.

"Oh, yeah," I say, remembering the sensation and...*surprisingly, not regretting it.*

He kisses my temple and says, "I don't regret it either, omegababy." A shiver runs straight through my pussy at the nickname.

"Chris lectured us on the dangers of UTIs during intense heats, so... they showered in the ground-floor gym."

I don't like it. At least Finny still smells like Finny, though.

I pull his arm closer to my face.

"Sorry, my love, I'll be bathing with you."

"Please stop reading my mind."

"Stop talking to me through our bond then," he smirks.

Can you hear me right now, you sexy thing?

"Yep."

How 'bout now?

"Yep."

Okay, this is gonna get me in trouble.

"Probably," he says, kissing me on the nose.

I'm prepared to fight them on this—my scrappiness can't be so easily swayed, *UTIs shwoo-TIs*—when Preston approaches me to say, "Temperature's good. I can cool it down if the fever hits, though."

The steam rising from the water's surface carries the scent of something herbal. I inhale, and my muscles ache to sink into it.

A bath would be kinda nice, actually.

Chris puts down whatever heavy thing he's currently lugging around and says, "I'll turn off the water, Pres."

Preston replies, "Thanks. Leave the hose, though, so we can drain the tub later."

Chris nods, then asks me softly, "Do you need to go to the restroom first, Evelyn? Would you like me to carry you?"

I hate this part: having to be accompanied to the bathroom during my heat due to weak muscles and/or delirium. Jacob would always throw me on the toilet, run out of the room, then come back a few minutes later—often to me sprawled on the floor. Chris is a doctor, I'm sure he's dealt with worse, so I shouldn't be embarrassed, but I am.

But, he's a neurosurgeon, they don't do this kind of caretaking stuff, right?

He's looking at me with such deference that something inside me uncoils.

Chris won't be like that. He'll be kind. He'll be gentle.

I nod.

"Would you like a robe of your own?" Bob asks, already carrying something soft folded in his arms.

I nod again.

Finn loosens his hold on me, and together, they help me sit up. I'm acutely aware of my nakedness, but none of them stare or leer. Their movements are careful, clinical almost, but with an undercurrent of tenderness that makes my chest ache.

Bob unfolds the robe, and I catch my breath. It looks even softer than their robes. It's a pale cream color, with dozens of delicate burnt-orange foxes in various adorable poses printed around it.

Oh my fucking God, it's so fucking cute!

A sound escapes me—half squeal, half gasp.

They freeze, watching me with wide eyes.

"Do you like it?" Tim asks as if it wasn't obvious.

"It's perfect," I say, embarrassed by my childish reaction.

"Good, because we got a crate of them," Tim smirks.

I'm a grown woman—a CEO of a multi-million dollar gaming company, for God's sake. I don't squeal over cute things.

Well, maybe I do.

In fact, I squeal again when they help ease my arms into the sleeves. This time, the squeal comes with little feet kicks when the robe wraps fully around me.

Chill, Evie. It's just a fluffy bathrobe.

I pull it to my face, hiding within it, and giggle. I fucking giggle. And because I haven't embarrassed myself enough, I paddle my feet even more.

Shit, that was very un-chill of me.

But, when I peer from behind the robe's fluffy softness, no one is looking at me with that leer of someone annoyed at an omega for doing their omega thing. In fact, they are all looking at me with warm fondness. They look pleased with themselves. Like the ridiculous noises I'm making over this bathrobe are proof of a job well done. As if making me squeal happily was the whole goal.

But, on top of that, they're looking at me like I'm something precious even now, when I'm weak, puffy-eyed, and losing my shit over cute things.

The realization makes my chest ache. I almost squeal again at how fucking cute all these big, loving boy eyes are on me, but...*a girl can control herself sometimes.*

Sometimes.

Chris steps forward and ties the sash at my waist. "Your phone," Chris says, placing it in my hand. "The robe has pockets."

POCKETS!!!

Get it together, Evie. Almost all robes have pockets.

With a gentleness that belies his size, Chris slides one arm beneath my knees and the other around my back, and lifts me so that he's cradling me against his chest. I rest my head against the soft robe so I can feel the steady beat of his heart.

Cozy. Safe.

"I've got you," he murmurs, and I don't know why, but those three words make my throat tight.

Finn rises to his feet, stretching like a large predator and returning his mask to his face. He silently follows as Chris carries me to my executive bathroom next door to my office. His mask and fluffy black robe make him look like a hot Grim Reaper taking a spa day. It would be scary if he weren't so deliciously sexy.

My shadow.

And just as they have transformed my office, they've also transformed my bathroom. The lights are dimmed, and flameless candles flicker on every surface, casting warm light that dances over the marble countertops.

Chris carefully sets me on a padded bench that wasn't here this morning, then turns off the sink supplying water to the hose attached to it.

He returns his attention to me and crouches before me, his eyes are soft, his expression open, and if there were any last pieces of ice in my heart, he just melted them. "Evelyn," he begins, and something in his tone makes me pay attention. "I want to apologize for earlier. For barking at you."

Behind him, Finn leans against the doorframe, arms crossed, watching our exchange with unreadable eyes.

I can tell Chris has a whole rom-com speech written in his head, so I let him have his moment and don't interrupt.

Chris continues, "I was out of line. I was worried about you, yes, but...that's no excuse. I'm going to work on it—my, what was it you called it? 'Bullshit alpha hormones'?" A small smile tugs at his lips, and I'm startled into a laugh.

He takes a deep breath. "I know I have some work to do to be a good packmate. I've been a bit of a loner most of my life, and I'm not really great with people." He runs a hand through his hair, a rare gesture of uncertainty from him. "But I'm going to put in any work I need to so that I'm a good mate for you. A good packmate to everyone."

The sincerity in his voice makes my chest tighten.

He's...willing to work for me?

"I only ask two things," he continues.

I raise an eyebrow, curious.

Here it comes. Some alpha bullshit that pretends to be compromise, but it's really a ruse to get you to capitulate.

All alphas are the same. They manipulate. They dominate. They get what they want and use your biology against you. I can't let my guard down, or they'll destroy everything I've worked so hard for.

I hold my breath as he says, "First, that you keep telling me when I fuck up. Don't let me get away with it, even if I get defensive at first. Call me on my bullshit, no holding back, just like you have been. And second, that you give me time to get better. I won't always get it right immediately, but I promise I'll keep trying."

Wait...so...I don't have to change? He's going to? I can't have heard that right.

His lips quirk in a half-smile. "We can even do a quarterly performance review if that's what you want. I've heard you're quite thorough with those."

A surprised laugh bubbles up from my chest. "With metrics and everything?" I ask, playing along.

"Complete with goals and areas for improvement," he confirms, his eyes crinkling at the corners. "I'm quite good at meeting expectations once they're clearly established."

I laugh again. "Are you suggesting I manage your alpha tendencies like a direct report?"

"If it works," he says with a shrug. "I'm open to whatever gets the job done. You can put me on a performance improvement plan."

The teasing words hold a deeper promise that sends a shiver through me. I nod, overwhelmed by this new side of him, by all of this. "I think I can agree to those terms."

"Don't worry, my love," Finn's voice comes from behind Chris, smooth as silk but with an edge of steel. "I will make sure he never barks at you again."

Chris laughs, a sound that tries to be casual but doesn't quite succeed. His shoulders stiffen slightly as he straightens, turning to face Finn with a carefully neutral expression.

"Good to know we have accountability measures in place," Chris says, his tone light but his body and scent screaming, "Yes, Prime Alpha, please don't murder me!"

The sight of this huge man cowering at this pretty face is almost too much.

I reach out, touching Chris's hand. "Thank you," I say softly. "For carrying me. For apologizing. For..." I gesture vaguely in the air.

He turns his hand to capture mine, squeezing gently. "Always." He waits a beat, then asks, "Okay, we'll leave you to it. Do you think you can stand on your own?"

I nod, even as my muscles protest at the mere thought of standing. "Yes, I'll be fine." The lie comes automatically, years of refusing help making the words flow before I can stop them.

Chris smirks at me, assessing my lie but not calling me on it. He rises to his feet, gesturing toward something beside the toilet that I hadn't noticed before. "Okay, so, since you can stand on your own, you won't need this...but, for later, I want to show you this."

It's some contraption of steel bars and padded grips nestled next to the toilet against the wall. I have no idea what it is.

"What is that?" I ask, confused.

"It's a mobility assistance device," Chris explains. "With it, you can reach any space within the bathroom. It has hydraulics, controlled by this," he puts a remote in my hand, "that you can use to lower yourself on the toilet." He points at the buttons on the remote. "You know...not for right now...but later when you might need it."

I stare at the device, momentarily speechless. "You...installed a toilet lift in my bathroom?" I finally manage, my voice sounding small even to my own ears.

Chris smiles, a hint of uncertainty creeping into his expression. "Is it too much? I know how independent you are, and I thought...of all the things you might need help with during your heat, going to the bathroom would be the one you'd most want to handle on your own. I'm sorry! Did I assume? Was I doing that thing where I think I know what you want and you didn't? Shit...I'm sorry."

The thoughtfulness of it—the careful consideration of not just my physical needs but my dignity, my fierce independence—hits me like a physical blow. My throat tightens, and my face burns. I look at the ground shaking with...*Gosh, I don't know what this feeling is.*

Chris continues, misinterpreting my silence as anger. "It can be removed without damaging the fixtures or the wall."

I reach out and grab his wrist. "Chris," I say, meeting his eyes again. "It's perfect. I just...I can't believe you thought of this."

The worry that had wrought his face seconds ago is replaced by genuine pleasure. "Oh, well, I mean, I just thought. Well, I'm happy you like it. You like it, right?"

"Yes." I smile. "No one has ever..." I struggle to find the words; my usual vocabulary inadequate for this strange new territory of being cared for. "Thank you."

He nods, hopefully understanding what I can't articulate.

He stands and unhooks the hose from the sink, wrapping the end with one of the neatly folded hand towels on the sink. "You can wash your hands now...if you want..." he stammers. And unable to help himself, "but, um...you should."

I laugh, "Okay, doctor."

"The bath will be ready when you are," he says. "Take your time."

As Chris moves toward the door, Finn still looms in the doorway, his dark eyes fixed on me with an intensity that makes my skin prickle with awareness and horniness. Chris says, "We'll be just outside. Call us if you need us."

Finn locks eyes with Chris just for a moment, and Chris immediately stops, turning his eyes to the ground and bowing his head. "Finn," Chris says, his tone carefully measured as he looks toward the ground. "Please don't look at me like that. She needs her privacy."

Finn hasn't even moved or shifted his posture in any way that screams intimidation, but that slight eye contact has Chris looking like he might piss his pants. I can practically hear the game announcer say, "Alpha v alpha. Fight!"

"She'll be fine," Chris assures him, voice softening. "The bench is within reach of the support bars, and the emergency button is right there if she needs us."

Emergency button?

I follow his gesture to a small, red button.

Finn shifts as if he's going to stand at my side.

I shake my head.

"Alphababy," I say, the nickname slipping out without thought. "I'll be right back, okay? I need a minute alone."

"Of course," he says, voice low and rumbling. "Whatever you need." He seems so sad that something dawns on me.

"Wait...when you were watching me before...did you follow me to the toilet?"

Finn freezes, his expression shifting through surprise, pleasure, and then reluctant acceptance.

Yes.

He shakes his head.

"Did you just say 'yes' through our bond?"

Yes.

He shakes his head again.

"Ha! Two can play this game, alphababy!"

Chris just looks at me, confused, but doesn't press.

"I won't be long, just give me a minute, okay?" I say to my sweet shadow.

Finn nods. He steps out of Chris's way, then, reluctantly follows him through the door, pulling it closed while saying, "Don't let Preston take credit for those snacks. I texted him about them."

Snacks? Where?

The silence as the door shuts behind them is a comfortable hum in my head. I remain on the bench for a long moment, assessing my surroundings and taking in the other changes they've made to my bathroom.

Behind the toilet, a small wicker basket holds fresh underwear and slick pads. On the counter, my usual toiletries have been supplemented with an array of products I've never seen before, all with labels like "Omega Comfort Balm." I stand on wobbly legs and brace against the marble countertop to access the various items. I ooh and aah at them as if I were in a spa assessing its products.

I open the medicine cabinet to find an array of prescriptions, all with my name printed on them. I don't really know what any of them do, but there's a note on the inside of the door, written in Bobby's handwriting, that identifies what each one does and when they can be taken. It lists muscle relaxants for when the cramps become unbearable, medications for stimulating slick production if, God forbid, my heat lasts so long I stop being able to produce it, antibiotics, and more supplements than I care to read about right now.

Next to the bench is a machine I don't recognize. I press the button on top, and it plays sounds of rainfall and chirping birds. I inspect it further, and it looks like I can connect my phone to it.

Oh my gosh...did they think of everything?

I bend slightly to open the cabinet under the sink, expecting just to find more toilet paper and sanitary pads, but instead I find the most tear-inducing cache of Evelyn-themed supplies I've ever stumbled upon.

There are multiple baskets adorned with adorable pink bows. Some contain stacks of e-readers, tablets, portable gaming consoles, books, sketchbooks, and colored pencils. Others contain all my favorite snacks that I treat myself to on particularly difficult days. Every craving group is covered: sweet, salty, crunchy, and fluffy. But it also contains snacks I've never told anyone I enjoy—my guilty secret pleasures—like those weird pickles I love that are only carried by that one gas station and the chocolate truffles my neighbor makes from scratch. *Finn*. There's even a tiny fridge with more skincare products and snacks. And on top of the little fridge is a basket of adorable plushies.

These aren't necessities. They're not for my health or to make their lives easier when they're dealing with me during this whole thing.

These are...just for me...just because I might like them.

I sneak a chocolate truffle and snatch a cuddly fox, holding it to my chest as I sink back onto the bench.

I look around, overwhelmed by the evidence of their care. They've thought about my comfort, my dignity, my need for moments of escape.

This isn't just about managing my physical symptoms or satisfying alpha urges. This isn't about making sure I'm a non-hostile environment for the pups they're likely planting within me. This isn't so they can dump me in here and make me do my most intimate business by myself when I'm lucid.

This is a retreat, a sanctuary, a place I can go when I need time to myself. This is a room designed to allow me to maintain my comfort and dignity when I insist on taking care of myself.

I sit on a bench, running my fingers through soft fox fur and along my soft robe.

How did they do this all while I was sleeping?

Tears roll freely down my face onto the soft fur of the cute little fox at my chest.

These men—*my men*—have seen a truth I've been running from for years: that my fierce independence isn't just strength, but also fear.

Fear of relying on others who might leave. Fear of being vulnerable with alphas who might use that vulnerability against me. Fear of being the omega I was born to be, with all the biological realities that entail.

And instead of exploiting those fears or dismissing them, they've honored them. Created solutions. Built me a space where I can be both independent and cared for.

I'm not alone.

I don't have to be alone.

As I sit here, coming undone by a cute fox, a box of chocolates, and a toilet lift, the realization settles over me like a warm blanket: I want to be their mate, all five of them, in every sense of the word.

Not just to ride out my heat. Not just unofficially. But bonded—forever.

I want to give these men the parts of myself I've kept guarded for so long.

Officially a pack.

I'm going to let Chris and Preston claim me and mark me.

They can rut into me and bite me as hard as they want, because I know they'll never hurt me.

CHAPTER 15
Preston

I'm kind of lost in the love of the moment. Evelyn's in the tub, sitting in Finn's lap, with her head leaned back on his shoulder, smiling blissfully as we all dote on her. I've never seen anything quite as beautiful as Evelyn in this moment—eyes closed, lips curved in a gentle smile, head tilted back, resting on Finn's shoulder, who is undeniably beautiful as well. The water in the inflatable tub ripples with each small movement she makes, catching the office's subdued lighting and casting dancing patterns across her skin.

"Is the temperature still okay?" I ask, dipping my fingers into the water to check. I've added a special blend of herbs—lavender for relaxation, chamomile for inflammation, and several others that work in concert to ease the symptoms of heat.

Thanks for the assist, Derek.

Her hair, still dry, has been piled atop her head in a messy bun that Bob somehow engineered with deft fingers. A few loose strands curl against her neck, darkening with moisture. My knees ache from kneeling beside the tub for so long, but I wouldn't move if the building were collapsing around us.

Evelyn makes a small sound of contentment, something between a hum and a sigh. "Perfect," she murmurs, not bothering to open her eyes. "Everything's perfect."

Chris stands a few feet away, phone in hand, but his eyes never leave Evelyn. Even as he types, his attention remains fixed on her, as though some invisible thread connects them.

Tim kneels beside me, washcloth in hand, gently running it along Evelyn's arm. His movements are careful, reverent almost. Bob is on the opposite side of the tub, doing the same. Finn's under her, supporting her shoulders and occasionally lifting her so the betas can wash her, carefully avoiding their touches himself.

Chris steps forward, pocketing his phone. "Sorry about that. I had to email work to request emergency personal leave." He kneels at the edge of the tub, rolling up his sleeves. "And now I need to call my mother to ask her to feed my cats."

"You have cats?" Evelyn asks, sounding delighted by this mundane detail.

"Two," Chris confirms, his expression softening. "Buff and Nerf. Mane Coons, brothers, total assholes, but I love them." He pulls out his phone again, showing us two huge and adorable cats.

"You would have giant cats," I laugh.

"They make me feel...normal size," Chris laughs.

"Aww, they're cute," Evelyn says.

"Do any of you have pets?" Evelyn asks the rest of us.

We shake our heads.

She looks up at Finn, "What about you, alphababy?"

"I have plants," he says, kissing her neck.

"Plant daddy," Tim murmurs, his eyes lingering on Finn with unmistakable heat. Tim has been having a hard time looking away from Finn. And, if I'm honest, all of us have.

My phone buzzes, and I check it.

> MOM
>
> Sweetheart, Patricia from book club, her niece just moved to LA. Lovely omega girl, studying veterinary medicine. Should I give her your number?

I groan, then dismiss it. Your mom texting while you're doting on your omega is probably the most embarrassing thing that can ever happen.

"What's with the groan?" Tim asks.

"My mom, trying to set me up with some omega she knows again."

"Your mom's trying to set you up?" Evelyn asks, and there's something almost like jealousy in her tone.

I nod. "She's relentless. Wants me 'settled' with an omega and grandkids before she's 'too old to enjoy them.'" I make air quotes with my free hand, mimicking my mother's voice.

Her scent spikes—gingerbread and surprise. "You can tell her about me. And...this." She gestures vaguely at the room, at all of us. "If you want to."

I study her face. "You sure?"

"She sounds like she wants grandkids. And I'm..." She trails off, suddenly awkward.

"In heat and with so much alpha spunk in you, you're probably knocked up as we speak?" I supply helpfully.

She swats at my arm. "I was going to say 'potentially part of your future,' but yes, that, too."

Tim pauses his ministrations, expression turning serious. "Potentially?"

Bob leans in, "Evelyn, are you saying that you want us all to be a pack. Officially?"

"Yes," she says, leaning her head back. No coyness, no fight, just "Yes."

"You mean, like, move in together, all of that?"

"Yes," she says, once again, completely unguarded.

I'm still beaming.

"Where will we live?" Bob asks, and I can see the gears already turning in his head as he plans out our next sixty years together. I hadn't thought that far ahead, too caught up in the immediate needs of Evelyn's heat, but he's right. Logistics will eventually need to be addressed.

"Well, I like LA, but I can move here," I suggest, surprised by my willingness to uproot my life.

"But, what about work and your platonic pack?" Evelyn asks, turning toward me.

I just shrug. "I don't need to actually be in LA to do most of my work. I could go out there when necessary and do the rest remotely. And Talia was gushing just this morning about us all moving here...I'll figure something out."

She furrows her eyebrows, "You'd uproot your whole life to be with us?"

She looks kind of angry, like I've stumbled into a trap somehow. "Yeah, of course. It makes more sense for me to move here to be with you than for all of you to move out to LA. Especially given your company is here," I add, twisting my finger around to encompass the building we're in.

The anger in Evelyn's eyes melts. She leans forward to run her hands through my hair, stopping at my jaw and petting my ears with her thumbs. "Preston, you'd do all that for us?"

I look around at everyone. "Yeah, of course."

She kisses me hard. I'm not sure why I'm getting such an extreme reaction from her, but she's happy, and that's all that matters. Actually, Bob, Tim, and Chris are smiling at me, too—and I realize that matters, too.

Evelyn turns to Finn, and before she can ask, he says, "I go where you tell me, my love." This elicits a similarly happy reaction, and I would be jealous except it makes me happy, too.

Bob, still running logistics, adds, "Six people...That's a lot to house."

Evelyn shifts slightly in the water, sitting up straighter, energized by the conversation. "My place is big," she offers, then adds with a small smile, "But not that big. Plus, I...I kinda wanna get out of there."

Chris, Finn, and I growl, knowing it's likely because the place still smells like those fuckers we all have to murder next week when her heat is over.

She looks between us and asks, "What? What's that about?"

"Nothing, my love," Finn says. "You just reminded us of something we have to take care of."

She looks at Bob for clarification, and he does that "Bob caught in the headlights" thing he does when he has something he doesn't want to say.

I save him by changing the subject, "We could look for something together."

Chris, also trying to turn the subject from the murder we're plotting, adds, "Yeah, we could find something with space for all of us."

"And a yard," Evelyn adds, her voice taking on a dreamy quality I've never heard before. "I've always wanted a yard." She pauses, then says more quietly, "For kids. And a dog. I want one of those little ones with the long hair and grinch feet. What are they called?"

"Cavalier King Charles Spaniel," Finn says, still only ever speaking to her.

"Yeah, one of those."

She breezed right past that word 'kids,' but it sent a jolt through me. In fact, I saw every single alpha in the room lock in on it.

Children. Our children.

The thought of Evelyn rounded with pregnancy, of small beings who carry pieces of each of us—it's overwhelming in its intensity.

"You want children?" Chris asks. His tone is careful, neutral, but I detect a thread of hope running through it. He tries so hard to be casual, but his failure, like his size, is epic. This is a question that's been on all of our minds since we unleashed our loads within her. I respect an omega's right to choose what happens after her heat, but I await her response with bated breath because I want little baby Evelyns so badly my knot aches.

Evelyn nods, a blush spreading across her cheeks. "I do. I always have, I just never found anyone I wanted to have them with." Her eyes meet mine, then move to each of the others in turn. "Until now."

The simple declaration steals my breath. In fact, there's a shared gasp between all of us men, and I now know each man in this room's stance on our possible future family. I want to start planning where our pups will go to college, but I gotta be chill and catch my breath first.

Tim recovers first. "I'd like that," he says, then grins. "Though I'm a bit terrified at the prospect of raising a mini-Evelyn with your temper."

This breaks the tension, and Evelyn laughs, splashing water at him playfully. "Hey! I'm not that bad."

"Do we dare bring up the black pen with blue ink situation?" Tim reminds her, but there's only fondness in his voice.

"That was different. I was in pre-heat and under duress. And that pen was an abomination."

"And what's your excuse for the other three hundred and sixty days of the year?" Bob chimes in, dodging the splash Evelyn aims his way.

My phone buzzes again. It's another message from my mom.

MOM

I gave her your number. She's really excited to meet you.

God, Mom, of course she is. She's probably moving to LA to be an actress. How much you wanna bet her first question is if we're casting for Torchbearer 2?

I ask Evelyn, "You sure I can tell her?"

Evelyn nods.

PRESTON

Mom, Christmas is coming early this year. I found an omega. And a scent-matched pack. Will explain later.

Honey. I know I've been a bit persistent, but there's no need to lie to me.

I lean my head back and groan.

I am not going to sit here and text with my mom right now.

I toss the phone to the floor away from me while it buzzes incessantly.

Tim laughs. "You can't just text a smother something like that and not follow up. You know she's having a meltdown now, right?"

Evelyn giggles again. "My dads are the same way. Send her a pic."

I perk up. I've been wanting to take pictures of her all day. "Really?"

"Yeah, just like, let me approve it first. I can't have a future mother-in-bond thinking I'm...well, this."

Future mother-in-bond!?

"Um, okay. Smile then." I open the camera app, holding it out.

She hesitates, then cleans the corners of her eyes and fusses with her hair.

"You're perfect. Gorgeous," I say, kissing her cheek. She smiles a real smile when my lips touch her cheek, making the perfect picture.

I make sure the frame captures just our faces, nothing inappropriate. The resulting photo is surprisingly sweet—her hair mussed but her eyes bright, my grin wide and genuine.

She nods her approval.

I send it.

My thumb hovers over my pack's group text. "Can I show my pack?"

"Yes," she says, nuzzling into my neck and licking me. "Tell them I think they're fucking stupid to not want to eat up this hot chocolate. But thanks for being idiots."

"I'm not gonna say that."

"I know," she says, her head drifting back to Finn's shoulder.

I open another thread to my packmates and send the photo along with the message:

Thanks for the help, guys! It worked. We're gonna make it official!

"They're going to lose their minds," I tell her.

My phone buzzes.

MOM

OMG! Prezzy! I am so happy! Thank God! I thought you—

But before I can read the whole notification.

TALIA

Holy shit!! I told you you'd be okay! I knew a powerful omega like that would be into a simpy little bitch like you.

Evelyn chuckles as the texts flood in, each more embarrassing than the last.

I flip the switch on the phone that turns it to Do Not Disturb and toss it aside.

"Well, that's enough of that," I say, with a nervous laugh.

Evelyn laughs again and yawns, "I should probably tell my dads."

Chris walks away. "I've got to call my mom about the cats." I watch him dial with a tenderness I haven't seen in him before. For all his gruff exterior, the man clearly has a soft spot for his pets.

"Mom? Hi, it's me," he begins, his voice shifting to something gentler than his usual clinical tone. "I need a favor. Can you stop by my place and feed the boys for a few days? I've had a...situation come up."

We all pretend not to eavesdrop, but it's impossible not to in the confined space. Chris's voice carries as he launches into detailed instructions about feeding schedules, medication for Buff's arthritis, and Nerf's preference for having his water bowl placed exactly two inches from his food.

Tim catches my eye, mouthing "cat daddy" with an exaggerated swoon. I suppress a smile, returning my attention to Evelyn, who's watching Chris with undisguised fondness.

"Yes, they need to be brushed daily," Chris continues, oblivious to our amusement. "And Buff won't let you do it unless you let him sniff the brush first."

"Oh, about a week. Yeah, I'm sorry, I know it's short notice—" He pauses, listening to something on the other end. His eyes flick to Evelyn, a question in them. She seems to understand what he's asking and nods her permission.

"Actually, Mom," Chris says, his voice taking on a note of barely contained excitement, "I found her. The omega I told you about—the one I've been looking for. We're scent-matched, and she's in heat, and I need to stay with her and...my new pack."

Even from across the room, I can hear the exuberant response from the other end—a loud, joyful exclamation that makes Chris wince and hold the phone away from his ear.

"Yes, Mom, I'll bring her, them all, to meet you soon. No, I don't know when exactly." He pauses again, listening. "Yes, I'm sure it's her. One hundred percent."

The grin on his face is so large it looks like his face is split in two.

When he hangs up, there's a flush high on his cheeks that has nothing to do with the steam from the bath.

"Sorry about that," he says, returning to us. "My mother can be... enthusiastic."

Evelyn reaches out a wet hand to touch his arm. "Tell me about your mom—your family."

Chris settles more comfortably beside the tub, his expression thoughtful. "I have a rather unusual family structure," he begins. "My birth mom, who I was just talking to, is an alpha—she's the head of a pack of five alphas."

"Five alphas? Wow. That's—" Bob says, voicing what we're all thinking.

"Intense? Yeah. They're all doctors. So, big surprise, I'm a doctor now, huh? I fought against it as long as I could, but...my mom's bark is... whew. Anyway."

"That explains a lot," Tim says, gesturing vaguely at Chris's imposing frame.

Chris raises an eyebrow. "What does?"

"Why you're so..." Tim waves his hand again, this time encompassing all of Chris. "You know. Big."

Chris agrees with a self-deprecating smile. "Yeah, what do you get when you mate two alphas? Bigger alphas?" he laughs. "Mom is kind of a big deal. It's extremely rare for female alphas to get pregnant, but I've got seven siblings. Anyway...always have large shoes to fill...pun intended."

Evelyn laughs, the sound light and unguarded. "One of my fathers is an alpha, Dad. He's kind of intense, too. I have an omega father, Daddy, as well. He's intense, but in that smothering, translating everything Dad is screaming through their bond kind of way. I don't have any siblings. What about the rest of you?"

It's my turn next, and I feel a twinge of sadness as I speak. "My parents are both betas. Were. My father passed away last year."

"I'm sorry," Evelyn says softly, reaching for my hand. Her fingers are warm and damp from the bath.

I squeeze gently. "Thank you. He would have liked you. But…um. I'm the first alpha in the family line on either side. Mom has been obsessed with me finding an omega since he passed. She doesn't get the whole…alpha thing. She tries, though. I have three older beta sisters."

"Well, you know my parents," Tim says to Evelyn, but then to the rest of us, he says, "I've got a mom and dad. Both betas. And a little brother who's a beta. They live next door to Evelyn's dads. That's how we know each other. Evelyn's daddy babysat me when I was little. Our dads are best friends."

"Yeah, they're 'golf buddies,'" Evelyn says, emphasizing 'golf buddies' in this faux deep voice that must be an impression of her dad.

"I was adopted by pair-bonded omegas," Bob says, "Mom and Dad. They've been together a long time."

"Bob, that's all you want to say?" Evelyn asks, almost launching out of the tub at him.

Bob shrugs.

"Can I tell them, then?"

He nods and smiles.

She lights up. "Bob's parents actually were the first omega couple in Minnesota to get the right to be pair-bonded."

Tim exclaims, "What!? Bob! I didn't know that! Why didn't you tell me?"

Bob shrugs again. "I dunno…it just…"

I bet I know why: Bob forgets he exists when Evelyn is around. It's all Evelyn—there is no Bob.

"His parents are fucking icons. They fought so hard for omega rights," she says, petting his hand.

Tim laughs, "No wonder you're so good with omegas."

Bob blushes, not liking the attention on him.

All eyes turn to Finn, but of course, he doesn't even notice, or if he does, he doesn't show it. He's not going to talk unless it's directly to Evelyn. I tap Evelyn's shoulder and point at Finn.

"Finn, what about you?" Evelyn asks, taking the hint.

He says to Evelyn, not the rest of us. "I have an alpha mom and omega mom. Just the three of us—no pack."

"Kinda like me," Evelyn says, and he nods.

"Do they live in France, too?"

"No. They live in...where is it? Is Florida a place?"

Evelyn laughs, "Yeah, it's a state. Will they be happy if you move to the United States?" Evelyn asks.

Finn's smile is warm. "Ecstatic. I don't usually come to the United States unless I have to."

"Do you talk to them?" Evelyn asks, and there's something new in her voice—a shyness that seems out of character. "I mean, like, out loud."

"I only speak to you, my bond," Finn says, as if it's the most obvious thing in the world. "They get emails."

"One day you're going to talk to the rest of us, though, right?" I ask, and he doesn't answer, doesn't even look at me, but he does almost—almost—quirk a smile, so I take that as a win.

Evelyn sits up, suddenly serious. "I have something I want to say," she says. Her voice is steady but quiet, forcing us all to lean in slightly to hear her over the gentle lapping of the bathwater.

She looks directly at Chris, then at me. "Chris. Preston." The sound of my name on her lips sends a shiver through me. "I want you to know that...when you're ready...if you feel compelled to bite me, you don't have to hold back."

My breath catches. A mating bite—the permanent bond that would mark her as ours, that would forge connections no one could break.

"Tonight, next week, next year," she continues. "Whatever timing feels right to you. And when your ruts kick in..." She pauses, drawing a deep breath. "I want you to go full rut. I don't want you to restrain yourselves. I want us to be an official pack. Forever."

Forever. The word echoes in my mind, expanding to fill every corner of my consciousness.

"Evelyn," Chris breathes, his voice rough with emotion.

"I need to thank all of you," she says, looking at each of us in turn. "For caring about me so much. For understanding me so completely in such a short time."

Her eyes grow bright with unshed tears. "I didn't realize how much hatred I had for alphas until...I found some I don't hate. I'm sorry that

I've taken that out on you. I'll work on it. I promise. But when I was sitting in the bathroom earlier, looking at everything you've all done for me—that's when I knew this fated scent-match stuff is real."

She reaches out, her wet hands finding mine and Chris's. "You're all my fated mates. And I want everything that means. The good and the bad, the easy and the hard. All of it."

CHAPTER 16
Preston

I can't stop smiling. My cheeks actually ache from it—muscles straining more than they do even when I'm posing for movie premieres or photoshoots. I know it means I must look ridiculous—that raw, goofy, uncontrollable smile my agent warned me never to show anyone—especially from my left, which Evelyn currently is looking at me from...

But I don't care.

Forever. She wants me.

Forever.

The word blooms from my chest, like sunshine breaking through clouds of my heart that I didn't even realize were there.

My hands tremble where they rest on the edge of the tub, and I stare at her in pure wonder, my hot chocolate scent puffs from me in big, soft, loving plumes, turning everyone to me; even Finn glances at me momentarily.

The playfulness in Evelyn's eyes dissolve, replaced by something darker, more intent. Her scent thickens to match mine, gingerbread notes intensifying to an almost painful sweetness that makes my throat constrict.

Mine.

She leans forward in the water, removing herself from Finn's lap to kneel in front of me. Finn frowns as she slips from his grip, but he glances at me, then leaves the tub and accepts a towel handed to him by Bob.

She's in my face now, running her thumb along my lower lip, parting my mouth slightly. "Preston, has anyone ever told you that you have the most perfect teeth?"

I laugh, self-conscious now. "Well, yeah. They're veneers."

"Mmm," she hums. "Movie star teeth. So white. So straight. So pretty."

I laugh again.

But Evelyn isn't laughing. Her gaze remains fixed on my mouth, and the intensity in her eyes makes something hot and electric shoot down my spine right into my balls.

Her gingerbread engulfs me, wrapping me in its possessive embrace.

"Sexiest Man Alive 2012," she says, leaning further out of the water and pressing her thumb against my canine, testing its sharpness.

It was 2014, actually.

Her breasts are no longer submerged; they now rest on the edge of the tub. I grip them, running my thumbs between them, recalling when I used to long just to get a peek of this spot. She leans her head back, moaning as I squeeze, thrusting herself against the edge of the tub.

Her head snaps back in place. "Can movie star teeth even make a proper bond mark?" she wonders aloud, her voice taking on a dreamy, almost detached quality. "Like...do the veneers block it from working?"

Shit? Do they? The dentist would have told me if they couldn't make a bond bite, right?

I look to Chris, panic overriding lust. "Chris!?"

But I don't hear his reply, because Evelyn growls, "Why don't we find out?" Then she replaces her thumb with her tongue, running it slowly, deliberately across my teeth. I feel the wet heat of her mouth, taste her sweetness, and a wave of possessive hunger that makes my vision narrow surges through me.

"Oh, babygirl," I manage, the words barely more than a growl.

Her heat is intensifying, the scent of gingerbread now thick enough to taste. My own body responds, hot chocolate notes rising from my skin, meeting her sweetness in the air between us. I feel lightheaded, my thoughts growing sluggish as biological imperatives begin to override rational thought.

Her eyes meet mine, conveying pure, unfiltered need—her heat taking full control. "Mine," she says simply.

With a jolt of strength, she grabs the collar of my robe and pulls. I topple headfirst into the tub, water splashing violently over the sides as my body crashes into hers and the edge partially crushes under my weight.

For a disorienting moment, I'm underwater, eyes burning against the various oils within it.

Then I'm surfacing, sputtering, only to find Evelyn already straddling me, her hands fisted in my soaked robe, face inches from mine.

"Babygirl—" I gasp, startled, flailing ungracefully, and trying not to drown, but the rest of my sentence evaporates as she kisses me with bruising intensity.

Her mouth finds mine in a kiss that's less a meeting of lips than a violent claiming. She bites my bottom lip hard enough that I taste copper, and the pain-pleasure of it sends a shock through my system that silences every thought except:

Her.

My head smacks against the edge of the inflatable tub as she pushes me backward and tears at my sodden robe. I'm submerged as her nails scrape across my chest, my stomach, lower, everywhere. My blood rises in the water swirling above me as it reaches for her—even it knows who it belongs to. It blooms into a bouquet of roses that I present as a courting gift just for her.

Hers.

All of me is hers.

Reaching for her always.

My fingers sink into the flesh of her hips, my thumbs between her legs, as I try to line up with her.

She pulls me up. I gasp for air, but her mouth covers mine, and she takes my breath away—like always.

So perfect.

I'm dimly aware of voices around us, but they're distant, unimportant.

All that matters is Evelyn.

The warmth of the water.

The warmth of her. The joining of our bodies.

Her hand grips my shaft, violent and hard as she positions me where she wants me.

Take what you want from me. Take it all.

When she sinks onto me, taking my full length inside her with one fluid motion, my vision blurs at the edges. My cock explores the depths of her, hitting that spot I am so fond of—the one that makes her wail out my name, sending a vibration through the rest of my body, and letting the rest of my body know that every square inch of me is hers.

All hers.

Forever.

When those perfect lips kiss against my knot, and I don't think she could feel better, they open up, allow my knot to enter her with a moment of resistance, then a pop. And when those perfect lips are now at my hips, a sound escapes me, making bubbles fill my vision, but...

Oh, I'm underwater.

She pulls me up again, and my lungs beg for air, but the rest of me begs for her. I cover her body with kisses, each place my mouth touches providing the most perfect balm to the burn in my lungs.

My hands roam down her back as I find the cheeks of her ass. I grip them hard as this perfect creature moves up and down my shaft.

She wails, wrapping her arms around my neck, and kisses a spot under my ear.

A sound escapes me—something between a growl and a whimper—and I feel her smile against my throat.

"You're mine," she says, her voice barely recognizable—deeper, rougher. "Say it."

"Yours," I gasp as she moves faster, setting a punishing pace. "All yours."

The water sloshes over the sides of the tub and pounds against us as our bodies collide, the rhythmic waves ebb and flow with each pop of my knot.

She pushes me down to get the friction she requires, and my head is underwater again.

Physicists got it wrong. There is a center of the universe—it's her. Because as she rides me, an explosion of heat in my loins expands outward, birthing new universes as stars explode into existence behind my eyes.

She's clawing at me, pulling me toward her so she can lick the hot chocolate off my neck. I gulp air, only to be pushed down again as she rides me with single-minded determination.

I break the surface again, gasping, only to have Evelyn's mouth crash against mine, stealing what little air I've managed to claim.

I'm drowning in her—in her scent, in her heat, in the actual water that keeps closing over my head as she presses me down, down, down.

I don't care.

If this is how I die, it will be worth it.

I'll lock my knot into her and shoot the last living remnants of myself into her. Her womb will carry on my legacy.

As her body tenses, I can tell I'm hitting exactly where she needs, so I let her hold me here as long as she desires.

Underwater, everything is muffled, dreamlike. Evelyn above me is a shimmering vision through the disturbed surface. Her breasts bounce as she rides atop me.

Perfect.

I should be concerned—some distant part of my brain registers that I can't breathe, that I should want oxygen, but the only 'O' I care about is hers.

So fucking beautiful.

The pressure in my lungs builds, but it's matched by the pressure building within her, a coiling tension that promises explosive release.

She comes hard, squeezing me, milking me, and I've fulfilled my life's purpose.

Just as black spots begin to dance at the edges of my vision, strong hands grab my shoulders, hauling me upward. My head breaks the surface, and I gulp air reflexively, even as Evelyn makes a sound of frustration at the interruption.

"For fuck's sake, Preston, breathe," someone—Chris, I think—says near my ear. "You're going to drown."

But Evelyn is still moving on top of me, still chasing her pleasure, and my body responds to hers with a mindless intensity that leaves no room for concerns about trivial things like survival.

I reach for her, pulling her closer, ignoring the water that sloshes over us both.

She's pulled from me. The beautiful heat of her is no longer around my cock.

"Evelyn, you're going to kill him," someone says, I don't know who.

I flail, coming up for air.

Babygirl, where'd you go!?

My cock aches for her.

I growl, low, deep, desperate.

"LET HER DO WHAT SHE WANTS!" I bark at no one.

"Don't fucking bark at Bob," someone says.

Then she's back!

Her body is on mine, we meld, we are one, two souls connected in heat and love and water.

"Bob, are you okay?" I think I hear someone say.

"Get them out of the tub before they kill each other," someone else says.

Hands are grabbing us both now, lifting us bodily from the water.

I fight them instinctively, unwilling to be separated from Evelyn even for a moment. She seems to feel the same, her legs locking around my waist, her arms around my neck as they haul us from the tub.

We're carried, still entangled, dripping wet, and half-clothed, to a pile of soft blankets.

It smells like my Evelyn. Like my pack.

Oh, it's the nest.

I immediately roll, pinning Evelyn beneath me.

She welcomes the change, arching up to meet me as I thrust into her again. Her hands are everywhere—pushing my soaked robe off my shoulders, sliding up my chest, tangling in my hair.

The scent of gingerbread is overwhelming now, filling my lungs with every breath, coating my tongue, seeping into my very cells. My own scent rises to meet it—hot chocolate, rich and dark, the two mingling to create something intoxicating and delicious.

I am no longer Preston Geist. I am nothing.

Not nothing. I am hers.

I am alpha. She is omega.

We are one.

My thrusts grow harder, more erratic, driven by instinct rather than conscious thought.

Evelyn meets each one with the same force, each thrust accompanied by a snarl and a gasp.

Her nails rake down my forearms, taking flesh with them.

Take it all, my love.

Take all of me.

The pain is distant, irrelevant, just another sensation in the overwhelming flood of input.

I surge forward, wrapping my arms around Evelyn's waist and pulling her tight to me. She wraps her legs around me, and I kneel, rutting into her as she sucks on my neck.

"So fucking yummy!" she moans into my neck.

I lick her. "Fucking yummier."

Mine.

Fuck.

Breed.

All I can do is feel—feel her heat against my chest, the deep heat within her, the heat of her breath against my neck, the heat of her tongue, and the searing heat of her nails raking down my back.

I thrust into her, giving her as much of myself as I can, but it's not all of me. My knot swells, catching on her entrance with each thrust, telling me there is more of myself I can give her.

"Alpha," she gasps, the word broken and perfect. "My alpha." The sound of her voice claiming me tips me over some invisible edge.

"Your alpha," I growl.

My vision narrows, tunneling until all I can see is Evelyn—her throat, her shoulders, the perfect juncture where neck meets collarbone.

The spot calls to me, demands my teeth.

"Mine," I growl.

"Yes," she agrees, tilting her head further, offering herself to me. "Yours."

Evelyn whimpers, her body trembling beneath mine, her inner walls clenching around me. She's close—we both are—teetering on the edge of something monumental.

"Please," she begs, and the single word contains universes of need.

I bend my head to her neck, inhaling deeply, letting her scent guide me to the perfect spot.

But at the last moment, my instincts direct me lower—to the soft swell of her breast, just where the fabric of her blouse always strains slightly during meetings, teasing and never revealing.

The place my eyes have been drawn to since the first moment I saw her. The spot I've thought of every time I've stroked my cock since I met her.

My teeth sink into the soft flesh, and the world explodes into light and sensation.

My tits now!

Fuck you, blouse!

You can't fucking stop me!

Evelyn screams, her body convulsing around me as her orgasm hits. My knot locks fully inside her, and my own release crashes through me with an intensity I've never experienced before. The air my lungs so desperately fought for earlier escapes me in a moan, through teeth gripped on flesh.

And with each thick rope I shoot within her, I feel a bond snap into place. Like a firework of consciousness, sparking through me. Bob. Finn. Tim.

Then, with perfect clarity, I see her. I know her.

I am hers.

She is mine.

We are one.

All of us, a pack.

Their love, their anxiety, their confidence...all of it is mine. All of me is theirs.

CHAPTER 17

Tim

I fall back, the shock of the bond snapping into me, literally knocking me on my ass. Overwhelmed by the sudden awareness of yet another alpha's emotions layered atop my own. My vision goes black around the edges, senses tunneling on Evelyn, as I feel them, all of them, and our collective orgasm. Well, almost all of them. *Not Chris...*

When my vision returns, I'm left here, knocked on my ass with bathwater, sweat, and jizz soaking my robe, panting. My hands tremble, and my knees are weak, but I'm at least able to get a grip on reality again.

Preston and Evelyn are locked by knot, tangled limbs, and roaming kisses. They're soaked on the nest, riding the afterglow of their coupling. Finn is bracing himself against the bookshelf, and Bob is already on his feet, scrambling for towels. Chris, unbonded, has maintained his composure. Well, not composure exactly...he's lashing out, flailing against the fear he experiences from loss of control. I don't need a bond to sense it.

He paces at the edge of the nest, a medical bag already in hand. "Jesus, Preston, she practically flayed you," he says, gesturing to the bloody scratches covering Preston's shoulders and arms. "Once you're disengaged, I need to dress those wounds."

Preston's coming to his senses, but still dreamily stroking Evelyn's hair with reverent fingers. He mumbles into Evelyn's neck, "Worth it." His eyes drift closed, a smile of pure contentment on his face.

I'm finally able to stand, knees still wobbly. Bob has reached the nest and kneels next to Evelyn and Preston. "Here," Bob says, as he approaches the tangled pair. "Let me dry you off, boss." There's something in his voice, and his scent carries an undercurrent of something sour.

I reach through our bond, first Evelyn, then Bob, and feel it, too: hurt, sadness, anger.

Chris isn't willing to let it go. "Preston, you can't let the rut take hold that hard. She was going to drown you."

"Would've died happy," Preston interrupts, opening one eye to grin lazily at Chris.

"Har har, Pres. The joke is getting old." Chris practically growls. "But, that's exactly my point! You would have died!"

Preston laughs, shrugging, "That's what alphas do: die for their omega."

He has a point. That is what alphas do: go all in, consequences be damned. Die for their omega.

Right?

Chris sighs, throwing his hands up in defeat, "Not like that, you airhead! Die to protect, not die stupidly in a bathtub while she's riding your cock. Or die from sepsis!"

Preston just puts his head deeper in her neck, "Same difference."

Chris gives up, "There's no getting through his rut haze right now."

"He can't help himself," I say, finally standing, though I'm not sure why I'm defending Preston.

"This is why alphas shouldn't let themselves go full rut," Chris says, his voice dropping lower. "They can't help themselves. That's not romantic—it's dangerous."

Now I understand why Chris gets so much anxiety around letting himself embrace his rut.

Bob drapes a towel across Evelyn's back, patting her skin with gentle motions. She hums in response, nuzzling deeper against Preston's neck, seemingly oblivious to anything beyond the man she's locked to. Bob works methodically, drying what parts of Preston he can reach without disturbing their position.

Preston blinks up at him, eyes still glazed but slowly clearing. His arms tighten around Evelyn, who remains sprawled across his chest, their bodies locked together by his knot.

"Bobby," Preston whispers, recognition dawning on his face. "I—did I bark at you? I'm sorry, I didn't mean—"

Bob shakes his head, cutting him off. "It's fine. Heat of the moment."

Chris is still pacing, grumbling, medical kit in hand, and Finn inches closer to the nest, his movements grabbing my attention. He's stunning. Beautiful. Exudes power. Makes you want to get on your knees and do whatever he wants. *Our Prime Alpha.*

But...

The bond between us thrums, coursing his anxiety through Evelyn right into my chest. Like a digital package of anxiety pinging through the ether of our network, at which Evelyn is the central hub.

He looks so composed. So in control. But he's terrified—always.

Has he always been like this? Or is it just due to current circumstances? Was that beautiful, confident boy band frontman always screaming with this much fear?

"Finn?" I call softly. "You okay over there?"

He doesn't turn, doesn't acknowledge me, but I feel him chanting through out bond, *'I'm fine. She's fine. I'm fine. She's fine. I'm fine. She's fine. I'm fine.'*

I look between these three alphas and reflect on who I thought they were before I knew them.

Is this what it means to be an alpha?

Dying for your omega's orgasm? Losing your mind to rut? Barking at your friends?

Losing your mind due to your own power? Losing your mind to your own size?

I always thought I wanted to be an alpha: bigger, stronger, able to make other people do what I want with just the sound of my voice.

Alphas always seemed so...sure of themselves.

But, they're not—at least my alphas aren't.

They're just better at faking it. Their enormous size and their pheromones just make better masks.

But now, seeing Preston's body marked with the evidence of his complete surrender to instinct, feeling Finn's barely-contained panic at the thought of losing control himself, seeing Chris panic because his packmates aren't falling in line—I'm struck by a profound sense of relief.

I wouldn't want it.

I wouldn't want to be the kind of alpha who drowns himself to please his mate, who loses all reason in the face of desire. I wouldn't want to be in constant fear of what might happen if I let go. I wouldn't want the responsibility of containing something so powerful it could hurt the people I love. And I wouldn't want to be so big that I'm afraid I'll cause harm, even when I'm trying to protect.

My beta nature has always felt like something less-than. But now I see it for what it is: a balance. I can support my pack without the crushing weight of alpha responsibility.

Chris stops his pacing to kneel beside Evelyn, examining the bite mark on her breast. "At least he got a clean bond mark," he says.

Preston stirs, eyes fluttering open. "Looks like movie star teeth can get the job done. I was worried for a minute there," he mumbles, sounding more like himself.

"Your teeth are fine," Bob says, his voice still carrying that hurt edge. "Your self-preservation instinct needs work."

Preston grabs his knee and says, "Sorry, Bobby, truly," and I can feel the deep sincerity of it stream through Evelyn to me. Bob gives him a tight smile, and I can feel him accepting Preston's apology in the same way as he leaves the nest, depositing the towels in a bin.

Preston's eyes are clearing, awareness returning to his face as he gazes down at Evelyn. The transformation is fascinating to watch—the wild, drowning man from the tub slowly becoming the beautiful movie star the world knows him as.

Evelyn, though, shows no signs of coming back to herself. Her eyes remain unfocused, her movements driven purely by instinct.

I can feel the difference through our bond—Preston's thoughts becoming more coherent while Evelyn's remain a swirl of heat-fueled need.

In one fluid movement, Evelyn braces her hands against his chest and flips their positions, rolling them so that Preston lies on his back with surprising strength. She pushes herself upright, straddling him and managing the impressive feat while they remain connected by his knot.

Preston gasps as his back hits the blankets, his wet hair splaying across the nest.

"Oh," he breathes, looking up at Evelyn with wonder as she straddles him. "Hello there, babygirl."

The blankets beneath them shift with their movement, revealing more of Preston's ravaged skin.

"Christ," Chris mutters beside me. "She really did a number on him."

Blood seeps from the scratches, but Preston doesn't seem to notice or care. His focus is entirely on her. "You're amazing," he tells her, eyes never leaving her face. "So strong. So powerful. Look what you do to me—I'm yours, completely yours."

She shifts restlessly atop him, her body seeking more despite their already intimate connection, trying to get friction on the knot locked within her. She's not able to move enough, locked in this position, and needs release, not from him exactly, but from the pain of orgasms still built within her.

For a moment, I think she's finished, but then she screams, "MORE."

The demand hangs in the air between us all. Preston, still knotted inside her, can't possibly give her what she's asking for. He looks up at her, a flicker of helplessness crossing his features—he wants to satisfy her, but he's physically limited by their connection.

This is why packs exist.

This is why packs form around omegas.

They need more than one alpha can give.

And even betas like me have our place, which I'm realizing is more essential than I thought.

Her eyes, wild and heat-glazed, find mine across the room. The intensity of her stare pins me in place, stealing my breath.

Before I can think too much about it, I'm moving forward, my hands already working at the tie of my robe. Something primal and instinctual guides me—not the mindless rut of an alpha, but something equally powerful: the desire to care for my pack, to meet their needs. The fabric falls open, then slides from my shoulders to pool at my feet.

"Tim," Preston gasps, relief mingling in his voice. "She needs—"

"I know," I say, approaching the nest. I position myself behind Evelyn, my hands finding her hips just above where Preston holds her. I kneel behind Evelyn in the nest, my chest against her back, my lips finding the curve of her shoulder. "This what you want, Evie?" I murmur against her skin.

Her head turns toward me, eyes finding mine with surprising clarity given her state. She nods, reaching out one hand while the other remains braced on Preston's chest. "Tim," she moans.

"I've got you," I whisper against Evelyn's neck, pressing a kiss to the spot where her pulse jumps beneath her skin.

She turns her head, seeking my mouth with hers. I kiss her deeply, tasting Preston on her lips, tasting her heat and need.

"Please," she breathes against my mouth.

My hands slide through her ass, feeling the slickness there. "You want this?" I ask.

She pushes back against my fingers, impatient and demanding. "Yes," she moans.

I grip my cock in my hand and slide it through the slick of her perfectly lubricated ass. "Oh, Evie, you feel so good," I say, unbelieving how slick omegas can get. "You want me to fuck that perfect ass?" I stop, right at her back entrance, and feel it, beckoning me to push forward.

Evelyn answers by pressing back against me with a whine. Preston's hands find her hips, steadying her as I position myself. Our eyes meet over Evelyn's shoulder. When I finally push forward, entering her body while Preston remains locked inside her from the front, the sound she makes is shocking in its intensity. I press forward slowly, carefully, giving her time to adjust to this new sensation. She whimpers, her body trembling between us, but there's no pain in the sound—only desperate need.

It's tight—almost impossibly so—but her body accepts me, drawing me deeper.

I can feel Preston through the thin membrane separating us, feel the throb of his knot where it locks him inside her. His hands find my wrists where I hold Evelyn's hips, a silent communication of trust and encouragement, as he helps guide me within.

"That's it, Tim," Preston encourages, his hands now moving to caress Evelyn's breasts as I begin to move within her.

"Look at you, babygirl," Preston gasps, returning his attention to her. "So beautiful. So perfect."

The sensation is strange and wonderful, this most intimate connection with both my packmates at once.

"My gorgeous omega," Preston murmurs. "Taking what she needs—what she deserves."

Evelyn and I reach for her clit at the same time, and for a moment, she squeezes my hand as if thanking me.

Preston pinches her nipples now, rolling them between his fingers with just enough pressure to make her gasp. "Is this what you need, babygirl?" he asks, voice husky with renewed desire.

I establish a careful rhythm, mindful of Preston beneath us. Trying not to get too lost in the sensation of her, knowing I need to pace myself if this heat wave is anything like the last.

"Yes," she hisses, her body trembling between us.

"We've got you," Preston assures her, increasing the pressure of his fingers on her sensitive flesh. "Whatever you need."

"My boys," Evelyn gasps. "My perfect boys."

The three of us find a rhythm together, Preston guiding from below, me setting the pace from behind, Evelyn caught between us in a pleasure so intense I can feel it reverberating through our bond. Her scent engulfs us, sweet and spicy, mingling with Preston's rich chocolate and my own spiced cranberry notes.

"Beautiful," I whisper against her neck, overwhelmed by the trust she's placing in us. "You're so beautiful like this, Evie."

"Beautiful omega," Preston continues, his fingers working her nipples in time with her movements. "My perfect mate. My everything."

His words seem to drive her higher. She moves faster, harder, her body demanding everything he can give.

"That's it," he encourages as she finds a rhythm that makes her whimper. "Just like that. You're perfect, babygirl. Absolutely perfect."

Her only response is a broken moan as her body tightens around us both.

I feel the moment her pleasure peaks. It ripples through our bond like an electrical current. She cries out, her voice raw and primal, as her body convulses in release.

I feel it as if it were my own—the intense pleasure, the release, the momentary sense of completion before need begins to build again. Preston groans beneath her, his body responding to hers even though he's already spent.

I continue moving, carrying her through the waves of her pleasure, but I hold myself back from my own release. There will be time for that, but this moment isn't about me—it's about Evelyn, about what she needs to weather her heat.

As her body relaxes slightly between us, I catch Preston's eye over her shoulder. There's a wealth of understanding in that look, a shared commitment to the woman between us and to the pack we've formed.

I may not be an alpha like him, but at this moment, I know my role is no less vital.

This is what it means to be a pack—not dominance hierarchies or designations of alpha and beta, but this: filling the spaces where you're needed, supporting where support is required, stepping forward when called.

And for the first time in my life, I feel perfectly, completely content with exactly who and what I am.

CHAPTER 18
Bob

I watch the hypnotic rhythm of Tim's hips as he takes Evelyn from behind while she straddles Preston, whose knot is locked inside her. And wait...

Wait until I'm needed.

Tim's hands grip Evelyn's hips, and he pounds into her with steady and relentless thrusts. Preston grins up at her like an idiot with those "movie star teeth" that I can't unsee now that Eveyln's brought it up. And Evelyn looks like the kind of goddess that would have convinced five men to drop everything else in their lives and commit, unquestioningly, to locking themselves in an office for a week to help her.

I'm entranced with the scene. The Christmas fucking feast of pheromones is so thick I can taste it. I pull my robe tighter and, perhaps for the first time in years, I let the tension in my shoulders relax. The desperate, needy, achy pull in my chest that draws me toward Evelyn is there, probably always will be, but it's eased by the knowledge that I'm not alone.

Chris stands beside me doing the same, but he isn't watching with the same appreciation I am. His jaw is clenched, hands flexing at his sides. A sharp pine scent, piercing, as if a tree just fell in the forest, pulls me from my lustful focus.

He towers over me, and when I look up to his face, all I see is worry etched there.

"Chris? You okay?" I ask.

"I'm scared," Chris whispers, an admission such as that would shock me from any other alpha, but not Chris. He always says he's not good with people, but he always tells you exactly what he's feeling. But, in this case, I didn't need him to tell me, because I can smell it on his pine and see it in his eyes.

He continues, "What if I go full rut and hurt her?" Now this does shock me, but it shouldn't. He's enormous—tall, broad, with hands that could easily span Evelyn's waist or crush my skull, and I know his size is something he's afraid of. I let myself really absorb our size difference. I'm the smallest man in the room and, while not as small as Evelyn, my perspective is definitely closest to hers. And I don't feel even remotely afraid of him.

Before I can say so, Chris continues, "You saw what happened to Preston. What if I lose myself like that and hurt her?" His eyes are still locked on the scene in front of us as he watches for even the slightest hint that he needs to rush in and provide assistance—sexual, medical, however.

"You're looking at what happened with Preston all wrong," I say, keeping my voice low.

In the nest, Evelyn throws her head back against Tim's shoulder, her lips parted in bliss. Preston's hands grip her hips, steadying her as Tim's movements grow more intense.

Chris shakes his head. "You saw him. He was...gone. Completely feral."

"And did he hurt her? Even once?" I ask, knowing the answer.

Chris pauses, his eyes squint slightly as he tries to assess the scene in front of us with new eyes. I turn my gaze back, but focus on Preston. His face is a study in concentrated pleasure and adoration as he looks up at Evelyn.

"No, but—"

"But nothing," I interrupt gently. "Preston would literally die before letting Evelyn feel a second of pain. That's not just Preston being Preston—" *a desperate simp just like me,* "—it's alpha instinct at its most primal level. The rut doesn't override protection; it amplifies it."

Chris doesn't look convinced, so I add, "Even if you lose control, you won't hurt her."

I'd like to see him fucking try.

Wha? Who was that?

Behind me, I sense Finn shift his position. I turn to look at him. He's leaning against the wall, seemingly disinterested in anything but Evelyn, with an air of aloofness that's simply a mirage created by his scent and beauty. The truth is, there's a continuous wave of anxiety flowing from him and funneling through our shared bond, as if our connection is a network of unseen tunnels explicitly designed for distributing his anxiety amongst the pack.

Chris's current spiral is churning Finn's emotions to an almost overwhelming level. Every time Chris's scent spikes or he mentions his worries over hurting Evelyn, a deluge of determined protectiveness bursts out of Finn. He might not seem like he's listening to or acknowledging Chris, but he's tracking him with a level of distrust that is understandable, given their limited familiarity. I'm having to actively dam back the torrent so I don't let it overtake my own feelings.

"I'm just so much bigger than her," Chris continues, his voice cracking slightly, as he keeps his eyes on Evelyn, Tim, and Preston. "What if I can't...control it?"

The scene before us feels like it should be enough to convince him. Preston isn't small himself, and Tim is almost as big as Chris is. Evelyn is currently being pummeled with more strong flesh than he has to offer alone, and she's perfectly safe.

I place a hand on Chris's shoulder, feeling the tension there. "Look at them," I say. "That's two huge men focusing every instinct on her pleasure and protection. When you go into a rut, you'll be the same. The fear you're feeling now? That protectiveness will translate perfectly."

Evelyn moans in a way that pauses our conversation momentarily as we both hold our breath and assess the scene. Tim's rhythm falters, and

Preston's worshipful whispers pause as he closes his eyes. They won't last much longer. It's almost time for us to step in.

Chris watches, his breathing uneven as he anticipates his turn coming up, as well. "How can you be so sure?"

"Because I can feel it. The first moment I met you, I smelled: protector. I don't know how to explain it. But I know you are safe and always will be. I'm not even remotely afraid you will hurt her or me...or anyone. But, more importantly, Chris, you've been rutting this whole time, and you haven't hurt her; in fact, you held back and waited until she was ready for you."

"I was holding back," he says.

"Yeah, but..." I pause. I don't think I can convince him that I believe he has fully lost himself a few times. I've seen the milky white beast in his eyes more than once, and instead of being afraid, I felt...safer.

I glance back at Finn—*time to change tactics.* "Alright, let's assume for the sake of the argument, you lose control, you try to hurt her. I'm still not worried."

Chris looks at me questioningly.

I tilt my head subtly toward Finn. "Contingency plan in the form of our newest pack member: Prime Alpha would stop you."

Chris follows my gaze to where Finn stands, seemingly aloof but undeniably present. He shudders and mutters, "Prime Alpha..."

I continue, "He might look like he's barely acknowledging any of us. But I can feel through our bond him tracking everything, ready to intervene if necessary." I look back and Finn, who doesn't acknowledge me with his eyes, but I know he agrees with me. "I think that's why he's here. Like fate, or whatever, sent an alpha powerful enough to freeze anyone, even you, with a bark. All he has to do is say stop, and you will, rut or not, he'll override your brain and stop you at the molecular level."

The concept seems to settle something in Chris, albeit slightly. His shoulders lower a little, though his hands remain tense.

I turn my head, catching Finn's eye across the room. For a moment, he actually looks at me directly—a rarity—and it stops my heart. *Stunning*. His expression barely changes, but I see the acknowledgement there before he covers his mouth with his hand—an unconscious gesture that I know serves as a replacement for the mask he wishes he had whenever someone looks at him.

I continue. "I trust you. Evelyn trusts you. All of us trust you. You need to trust yourself, Chris."

In the nest, Evelyn's movements are becoming more erratic, her breathing hitched. Preston's grip tightens momentarily, then relaxes, his focus entirely on her face—his knot is going to recede soon.

Chris nods slowly. "I just...the last thing I want to do is hurt her."

"And that's exactly why you won't," I reply, feeling the truth of it in my bones. "She wants you to let go. She said so. Look at her. She can take it. Not just take it, she needs it."

His posture relaxes, just slightly.

"Just breathe, Chris," I murmur. "When the time comes that you lose control, it will be okay. And we'll all be right here—ready to fucking murder you if you so much as split a hair on her head."

Chris laughs. "You gonna take me down, Bob?"

"Alphas aren't the only ones who'd die trying to protect their omegas," I shrug. He laughs again and puts his hand on my shoulder.

"Thanks, Bob. You really do always know exactly what everyone needs."

I grin. "It's my job." I, as much as everyone, know it's not really, but it's become a bit of a catch phrase at this point.

Tim's rhythm hasn't faltered, the steady slap of skin against skin filling the office as he continues to take Evelyn from behind, but his breathing is ragged, his jaw clenched with the effort of control. Preston shifts slightly beneath her, his expression changing from intense pleasure to that satiated calm of an alpha whose knot is going down. Evelyn's lust doesn't seem like it'll be breaking anytime soon, so I brace myself, ready to get tagged in.

Preston eases himself out with careful movements, and I feel a tightening in my gut as I anticipate what's coming next. The moment they disconnect, Evelyn lets out a whimper that strikes something in my chest—a sound of loss, of emptiness suddenly felt. Her fingers clutch at Preston's shoulders, her body trembling.

"Don't worry, babygirl," Preston murmurs, brushing sweat-dampened hair from her face with a gentleness that contradicts his imposing frame. "Someone's got you."

His eyes find mine over her shoulder, and a slight smile touches his lips. "You're up, Bobby." He slides out from under Evelyn, leaving her supported by Tim, who slows his movements but doesn't stop.

The nickname sends a familiar warmth through me. Evelyn's the only person who ever calls me Bobby, but I don't mind Preston using it. It's an acknowledgement of our kinship, and his subtle way of continuing the "Preston Appology Tour for Barking at Bobby" that's traversing through our bond.

The vibrator in my hand hums to life.

Best thing I ever bought.

I approach the nest, ready.

Kneeling before her, I catch her gaze. Her eyes are glassy with pleasure and need, lost to heat, but when she sees me, a flash of recognition and relief crosses through them.

Tim shifts his position and pauses his movements to allow me to ease the toy inside her.

I position the vibrator at her entrance, already slick and ready from Preston. I stroke it along her first, teasing, watching her shiver with pleasure on Tim's cock as goosebumps cover her flesh.

When I finally press it inside her, she gasps, then pulls me in for a kiss. I twist it slowly, watching her reaction, going where I can see it gives her the most pleasure, learning her body like I'm studying for the most important test of my life.

"That's it, baby," I murmur as her body accepts the vibrator. "I've got you now."

She reaches for me, untying the belt of my robe, then running her hands over my body.

Tim resumes his rhythm, now more measured, working in counterpoint to the vibrations.

I work the vibrator deeper, feeling her body accept it, watching the flush spread across her skin. The scent of her is overwhelming, gingerbread mixed with hot chocolate and spiced cranberries. It smells so fucking delicious.

Her scent intensifies with every passing second, and my mouth waters. With my free hand, I reach down and run my fingers through her. I pull my hand back and look at my fingers.

"Oh, baby," I moan before I suck my fingers. The flavor explodes across my tongue—sweet, complex, unmistakably Evelyn, unmistakably my pack. "You taste so fucking good."

I need more.

I lean in, face level with where the vibrator disappears into her beautiful pussy, ready to lap up the gingerbread and hot chocolate dripping out of her. I run my tongue over her swollen flesh, and groan as my tongue flicks over her clit. My lips buzz with pleasure as the vibrations of the toy travel through her to me.

She's so sweet. So delicious.

God, I love her.

I love them.

My own arousal is almost painful with want. I run my free hand along the length of her, coating my hand in her delicious slick. Without breaking the rhythm of my tongue, I coat my cock with her and groan again as the wetness spreads down my length.

I stroke myself absentmindedly, not really to come, but just enough to relieve the ache that was distracting me from my true purpose: her. I'm more focused on the sounds she makes as my tongue circles her clit, cataloging each of her micro-reactions, intent on maximizing the pleasure I bring her.

This all still feels like a dream. I've imagined this so many times. But none of the fantasies, none of them, compares to the reality of her coming apart under my tongue.

I increase the vibrator's power and feel accomplished when she jerks, then moans and grinds harder against my tongue. Her thighs tremble under her, and the pride radiates through me.

I lose myself in the rhythm of it, in the wet heat against my tongue, in the tremors that run through her body.

This is devotion in its most physical form.

My cock throbs in my hand as I pleasure her, my own arousal secondary but insistent.

Tim's movements are shorter and more controlled now as he rocks her into my face.

The vibrator hums louder as I increase the setting. The artificial knot expands inside her, mimicking what her body craves—what I can't give her.

My tongue moves faster, more deliberate.

Her fingers tangle in my hair, and the added connection makes me groan against her flesh and reflexively thrust into my hand.

"Bobby," she gasps, the name breaking on a moan.

I know she's close. I can feel it in the trembling of her legs, hear it in the pitch of her voice, and sense it in the change in her breath.

The vibrator pulses faster now, mimicking the final stage of knotting.

My jaw aches, but I don't stop. I couldn't if I wanted to. I look up to her, without stopping my ministrations. The muscles in her stomach clench and contract, her breasts bounce, and her head is thrown back on Tim's chest. Tim's chin rests on her shoulder as he kisses her neck. His fingers dig more assertively into her hips as he says, "Oh, God," in that way I know means he's close. His eyes meet mine, a silent communication passing between us, as he confirms what I already knew. He's close. So is she.

Good. A job well done.

They're so fucking beautiful like this.

The moment builds, her body tensing as the combined sensations overwhelm her.

I press the vibrator deeper, expanding the knot function to its fullest, but not yet locking it in place. Her body tenses, then shudders violently. She comes with a cry torn from somewhere deep inside her, her body clenching around the toy, against Tim's cock, against my mouth.

Her contractions pulse against my lips, and I have to push the vibrator in a bit more as her body threatens to push it out.

I don't stop, don't slow down, determined to give her everything she needs.

My own hips rock against nothing, my body wanting release that I won't give it because my body is not important in this moment.

As her breathing begins to steady, I ease the vibrator's intensity just a bit, but keep it in place, knowing she needs the fullness as she comes down.

I withdraw to my knees. My cock stands proud and thick, and the assistant in me preens a little at the accomplishment of pleasing my boss.

"You like my fat alpha cock, boss?"I ask, not expecting a reply, then add, "I'm going to knot you now."

She smiles and reaches for me, as she breathes out my name, "Bobby."

My thumb hovers over the lock button, but stops when she says, "I want your real cock."

My real cock?

The ache that's been persistently nagging in my aforementioned cock moves to my chest and catches in my throat. Warmth unfurls in my chest like a coil that's been tightly wound there for years.

My hands shake as I remove the vibrator, setting it aside.

Even surrounded by alphas, even with toys designed to satisfy her most primal needs, she wants me.

The real me.

She wants me.

I move forward, and Tim helps me move her to a position that will accommodate my height. He slows his thrusts so that they're barely noticeable, allowing me the opportunity to enter her.

With the same hand I held the vibrator, I grip my dick—it's heavy with want, but not nearly as heavy as the vibrator. Part of me wants to feel inadequate. But just as I told Chris he needed to trust her and trust himself, I need to do the same. She said she wants me, precisely as I am, and I will give it to her.

The first touch of my cock against her entrance sends sparks through every one of my nerve endings, thrusting a moan from deep within me.

I push into her slowly, feeling her body open to me, accepting me, embracing me, loving me. She's hot and wet and perfect around me, and I have to pause halfway to regain control.

The feeling is bliss—pure, uncomplicated bliss.

"You feel so good, Evelyn," I breathe, finally seated fully inside her. I rest my head on her breast, overwhelmed with my love for her and the pleasure she brings.

She cradles my face so that our eyes lock and brushes her thumbs across my cheekbones.

"Bobby," she whispers, "you need to come, too."

"Anything for you, boss," I murmur, turning to kiss her thumb.

"Not 'boss,'" she says, eyes still locked on mine. "Baby."

"Anything for you, baby," I smirk and kiss her.

The permission—no, the request—undoes me.

I move, finding a rhythm that's slow at first but builds quickly, each thrust more confident, more intent on experiencing her to her fullest.

Her body responds to each thrust, pushing back against me, demanding more. I give it to her, everything I have, everything I am.

Once we develop our cadence, Tim resumes his thrusts, matching our pace as we dance together as a team. I can feel him on the other side, pounding against me through the thin layer of flesh that separates her channels.

I lose track of time, lost in the rhythm of our bodies, in the increasingly desperate sounds we three make. The world narrows to just us, just this.

My pace quickens as I feel the familiar tightening at the base of my spine, the building pressure of release.

She pulls Tim's head to her shoulder, then mine to the opposite. Tim and I continue to thrust within her, our pace synced as we take her from both sides, and wrap our arms around each other.

When our arms squeeze tight, combining the three of us as a single pulsing unit, I am overwhelmed with my love for her. For both of them.

I kiss her cheek, tears welling in my eyes, "I love you so much, baby. I love you both so much."

Tim replies, his voice cracking, "I love you, too."

"I love you, too!" Evelyn says as her walls close in on us both, her orgasm waves through us.

"Evelyn," I gasp as the pleasure crests and breaks.

Tim follows us over, his movements stilling as he finds his release.

As I come inside her with shuddering pulses, I feel Tim do the same, not just through her walls but through the shared bond of my pack.

My pack.
My family.

CHAPTER 19

"You let it take you too far," I murmur, as I wipe antiseptic along a particularly deep scratch on his bicep. "The rut. You disappeared into it."

Preston's eyes, still heavy-lidded with satisfaction, meet mine when I apply a bandage to the wound. "Not as much as you think, doc."

"I watched you. You were gone." I tear open another antiseptic packet with more force than necessary, letting my anger out on it.

He doesn't flinch as the alcohol touches raw flesh. "I wasn't gone, Chris. I was...present. More present than I've ever been." His voice drops lower. "I was there, in the moment with her. Not worried about the future. Not worried about the past. Just...present."

I ignore his words, focusing on a set of crescent-shaped indentations where Evelyn's nails dug into his chest.

"If you want to bond with her, you have to let it take over, Chris. You can't keep holding back," Preston says.

From the nest behind us, I hear the subtle shifting of bodies—Bob and Tim moving around Evelyn, their scents mingling with the lingering traces of release.

The air is thick with it, with them, with her.

That's my girl.

Mine.

I've known it since the moment I laid eyes on her.

I was young, tiny, powerless…except when it came to *Embrace the Suck*. At that video game, I was a god. I played games to escape my overbearing family— to escape my older siblings' pummelings (both physical and verbal). I entered the tournament, cocky despite my small size, eager to let the waves of fear radiating off my opponents wash over me. Back then, I craved fear from others, and games were the only thing I could do that instilled it in others.

How ridiculous it was…

I certainly got what I wished for.

I booted into the game, ready to dominate like always, and before I even reached the first weapon's cache:

KnightOfYore was slain by FoxyWig

I looked around the room, trying to spot who got me, but my avatar respawned, and I returned my attention to the game. I got a few kills then:

KnightOfYore was killed by FoxyWig

then

FoxyWig killed KnightOfYore with a slick grenade

and

FoxyWig showed KnightOfYour who's boss

over and over.

But it wasn't just me. Everyone. She took us all out at an unrelenting pace.

Brutalized.

When the last headshot took me out, I stood, throwing the

controller to the ground. "What the fuck!?" I screamed, my voice cracking. "Who is FoxyWig!?"

The alpha next to me snorted, "Sit down, shrimp."

I looked back and my screen only to see a pink character squatting over my corpse: teabagging me. A feminine giggle turned my attention to a player down the way. And that's when I saw her, the goddess in a fox scarf. She was beautiful—a woman, not a girl. Older than me and so out of my league it would have been embarrassing if I cared. I didn't.

I looked back at my game, my brain rewired, my life's path altered. I was no longer on the path my parents had laid out for me. I was single-mindedly following whatever path led me to her. When the screen faded to black, fading away her player character still teabagging mine, I thought:

One day, darling, you will sit on my face like that. Just wait.

At that point, I still thought she was a beta. But I didn't care. It didn't change the irrefutable fact that she was my fated.

My brutal beta beauty.

During the breaks, she sat on a beanbag chair with another beta, whom I suspected she was bonded to. He was large for a beta, really large, and really cute. Intimidating as fuck. Every time I approached them to talk to her, one of them would look at me, stop my heart, make a pathetic squeak escape me, and send me running to a corner to reformulate my next approach.

The tournament lasted way too long. It was wholly unnecessary. It was obvious who the winner would be after that first round, but I suspect those in charge of decisions wanted to give the others a chance to redeem themselves—they never did. By the time it was finally called, we were all exhausted. When we got our trophies, I stood proud next to her. She towered over me, and I looked up at her, thinking:

Angel. Perfect. Goddess. Mine.

Then anguish overtook her face, and she wailed out in pain. The memory after that is a little hazy, but I do recall my mind being consumed with the thoughts:

Not beta—omega. Mine. Breed. Fuck. Fuck. Fuck.

But I wasn't the only one thinking it. The others she had spent the last eighteen hours emasculating were thinking it, too. They sneered, surrendered to their rut, and braced to leap forward to dominate her as payback for dominating them.

Mine. Mine. Kill. Kill. Protect. Protect.

I stood as tall as I could between her and them and barked, "Don't fucking touch her!" But, it was the bark of a chihuahua, not an alpha.

Useless.

But the trophy in my hand wasn't useless.

I saved her. I protected her.

My parents arrived just in time to save me from being murdered, but not in time to save my two broken legs and dislocated jaw.

Worth it.

Wait—

A sound cuts through my thoughts—a soft, needy whimper from Evelyn. My head jerks up automatically, eyes finding her across the room.

Worth it...

I get it...

She's nestled between Bob and Tim, their hands stroking her gently as they all come down from their shared high. Her eyes are clouded with residual pleasure, but still seeking.

Still wanting. Still needing.

She needs me.

ME.

MINE.

I move toward the nest. Following the path she laid out for me twenty years ago: the path from me to her.

Gingerbread. Spiced cranberries.

I always wondered why my memory was so hazy. And all day I've been wondering how I thought the two scents were one. How could my memory be so confused?

Because...I had gone full rut.

I had lost control. On that day, the day she needed me, I lost control, and I was exactly what she needed of me...

I let my robe fall to the ground, cross the room, carried on limbs no longer mine to control—*hers*. They are hers. She pulls me.

Beautiful.

Perfect.

Mine.

Protect.

Love.

Forever. Always.

I'm not afraid anymore.

Bob shifts slightly to make room for me.

The smile she gives me tightens my chest, lurching my heart forward so that it explodes from my ribcage and lies before her as an offering.

My goddess. I am yours. Consume me.

I lower myself to one knee beside the nest, beside her, close enough to feel the warmth radiating from her skin.

I growl, "Mine!"

She smirks, says "There's my knight in shining braces," and reaches out for me.

I take her hand and mine engulfs hers. I turn her hand around in my much larger grip, feeling the delicate bones beneath the unthinkably soft skin. I look back at her face, expecting to see apprehension flicker across her features as my hand dwarfs hers, but instead her eyes soften.

Not fear. Happiness.

Evelyn, the woman who never backed away from a challenge, doesn't cower. How arrogant of me to think I could scare this fearless woman. The woman who brutalized a room of alphas for eighteen hours and simply giggled when they cursed her name.

Tim rolls away from her side, standing with a fluid grace that belies his recent exertions. "She's ready for you now," he says, putting his hand on my shoulder, kissing my cheek, and walking away to clean up.

No more hesitation.

I'll take what I want.

Because what I want is…

To love her. To love them. To help her.

The scent of her hits me full force—gingerbread and arousal and the mingled essence of our packmates. My mouth waters involuntarily.

She lifts to her knees, and I release her hand to lie beneath her. I gently spread her thighs wider so I can slip my head under her.

I told you, darling, one day you'd sit on my face.

The first stroke of my tongue against her swollen flesh draws a gasp from her lips...

...and my mind wipes.

Gingerbread. Wet slick. Gingerbread.

Delicate flower.

So gentle.

Cinnamon. Spiced cranberry. Hot chocolate.

Trembling.

Gentle flicks.

So wet.

Her taste fills my senses, sweeter and more complex than anything I've ever experienced. I lose myself in it, in her, forgetting everything but the need to bring her pleasure.

One finger in.

Ooooh fuck, so perfect.

Mine. Ours.

Suck.

Throbbing on my tongue.

Trace her. Map her. Memorize the perfection.

Legs clench my ears.

I increase the pressure of my tongue, circling her clit with deliberate focus.

Two fingers. Hook.

Wail.

Yes, my love, I know where you like it.

Three fingers. Four.

She moans. Her inner walls clench around me, hot and wanting.

Pulse on my tongue. Suck.

Thrust deeper.

She falls forward so that her face is on my stomach. She claws and kisses. It tickles.

Legs squeeze my temples.

Pulling me closer, I can't breathe. I don't care.

Worth it.

Hook.

Kiss. Suck.

Hook.

Delicate flesh fluttering on my lips.

Gentle. Rough.

She likes both.

Nails digging into my side.

"FUCK!" she wails.

Slick walls clenching around my fingers, pulling me inward, and pushing me out at the same time.

She lifts off my face, crawling, clawing her way across the mountain of my body toward my cock. She reaches it and sits on it, struggling with the angle, wiggling to get it inside her.

I sit up, hug her tightly to my chest.

Mine.

I bring her down with me so that we're lying on our sides.

I position myself behind her, aligning my body with hers.

So small. So tight.

She won't break.

I won't break her. I'll complete her. I'll help her.

I run my hand down the length of her, caressing her breasts, while I use the other to help her guide my cock inside her.

"So beautiful," I moan.

When her entrance aligns with the head of my cock, I press forward, slowly, but for the first time, without hesitation.

The initial resistance gives way, and I sink into her with a groan that seems torn from somewhere deep in my chest.

Oh, God. This is what I was built for.

I was given this size not so I can protect her, but so I can please her.

She's impossibly tight.

Every millimeter of flesh that combines with hers feels more perfect than the last.

So warm. So wet. So perfect.

The heat spreads through my veins like wildfire, sharpening my senses.

Her body yields, accommodating my size.

I'm not penetrating. She's engulfing. She's absorbing.

She's taking. I'm giving.

"Yes," she gasps, pushing back against me, taking me deeper.

I'm what she wants.

I'm what she needs.

I establish a rhythm, slow and measured at first, one hand gripping her hip to steady her.

The rut is still here, still primal, still taking hold of my mind, focusing on nothing but our joining and what she needs.

It's been here the whole time.

I just didn't realize it.

My pack: their scent surrounds me. Cradling me in their love. Their need.

My pack. Christmas.

"More," Evelyn pleads, reaching back to grip my thigh.

I pull out, and she whimpers, but I capture it with a kiss.

No, sweetheart, you'll never feel pain again. Not while I'm here.

She kisses me deeply as I settle her onto her back and re-enter her, hitting even deeper with this new position.

Her legs wrap around my waist, ankles crossing at the small of my back, pulling me in further.

My eyes lock on the curve of Evelyn's neck. I nuzzle the top of her head and breathe in her scent.

Filling.

Perfect.

Vision black. Eyes closed.

I moan.

My purr rumbles through the air.

Another moan, not mine, hers.

So beautiful.

So delicious.

I thrust forward, reaching the deepest, most perfect spot.

Rhythmic thrusting. Lost to it.

Grunts.

Wails.

Pleasure. Nothing but pleasure.

Her body tenses, vibrates, shakes.

Knot swelling.

Her walls clench around my shaft.

My knot pops in. Swells, locks.

She comes—her walls squeezing me, milking me, gripping me. The muscles within her constrict in a perfect wave, working together to pull me toward her.

Guiding me toward her.

Hot, explosive pleasure releases from me, rushing toward her, rushing into her, knowing the path it too has been destined to follow.

Gingerbread dances along her neck. *So alive.*

My teeth ache as I nuzzle into her neck. *So perfect.*

I lick the pulse thrumming in her neck. *So delicious.*

So beautiful.

So mine.

Bite. Claim. Mark.

Don't possess. Protect. Pleasure.

I bare my teeth and place them upon her flesh.

Her pulse jumps.

Pause—

No, I shouldn't. I can't. This isn't what she wants.

"Yours, Chris. I'm yours. Do it," she says, her voice rasping with pleasure. "Join us in bond."

I bite down.

Her pulse jolts through me, each pulse pounds in my ears, bringing with it new awareness:

Thump—Evelyn.

Thump—Tim.

Thump—Bob.

Thump—Preston

Thump—Finn.

Then an explosion of pleasure cascades through us all, connecting us, like a network of Christmas lights, all lighting up at once.

CHAPTER 20

Evelyn

I wake up with a swelling fire burning under my skin.

The world swims into focus.

It hurts. So much pain. Molten lava. Heat. Need.

NoooOOOOOOooooo!!!

My body trembles despite the warmth of bodies surrounding me.

Breathes on flesh. Heart beats soothingly.

But the heat—oh god, the heat—it's worse now, a desperate aching emptiness that claws at me from the inside.

I need...I need...

A large framed silhouette, outlined by the cozy, dim lights, crosses the room, robe falling to the ground—a purr: Chris.

Oh, whoa, he's handsome.

The heat melts me. *No...he melts me.*

My skin feels too tight, too hot.

An arm tightens around me. Sleepy voice says, "We got you, omegababy." White hair cascades around caring brown eyes and a beautiful face—low, sensual purr, followed by humming: Finny.

He's so pretty.

The heat melts me. *No...he melts me.*

A hand trails up my leg. Rough, sure...worshiping. "Oh, babygirl, it's okay. We're here." Movie star teeth flash a smile just for me—another purr: Preston.

Another pretty boy.

The heat melts me. *No...he melts me.*

A hand brushes hair from my face. A kiss to my temple. "We're here, Evie, don't worry." Tears are kissed from my eyes: Tim.

What a cutie.

The heat melts me. *No...he melts me.*

Ice cold wetness. "Do you want Chris first, boss?" Sweat dabbed from my brow with a cold washcloth: Bob.

Where'd all these pretty boys come from!?

The heat melts me. *No...he melts me.*

I gasp, "Yes!"

Chris hovers over me. "Evelyn," he whispers, a question and a statement all at once.

I don't answer with words. I can't. The lava roiling within me overtakes rational thought, leaving only instinct.

Snow. Fresh white snow. Shaking off pine needles. Cooling me.

My knight. My protector.

And now...suddenly...the heat isn't there anymore.

The pain is gone.

Now there's only need.

A need for closeness. A need for comfort.

It's insatiable. All-consuming. The drive to consume everything with my body consumes my thoughts.

I extend my arms to Chris, reaching for him, trying to pull him toward me and meld his body with mine.

The loss of contact makes me cry out, my flesh angry to be alone.

"Shh, I've got you," Chris murmurs, gathering me against his chest.

My body arches into his touch, seeking more contact, more pressure, more anything to ease this unbearable need.

"Please," I beg, my fingers dig into his shoulders. "I need—I need—"

He understands without further explanation, lowering me back into the center of the nest.

I'm vaguely aware of movement around us as the others swarm.

Hands, more than two, are everywhere at once—stroking my sides, cupping my breasts, sliding between my legs to find me impossibly wet.

I close my eyes, and someone slips their dick in my mouth. I suck, hard. But it's so small. And it beeps at me.

What the fuck?

I open my eyes. Chris is looking at a thermometer. "Shit, that's too high," he breaths.

Hey! Eyes on me, butthead!

He says to someone who isn't me, which really pisses me off, "Get the ice packs."

I whimper, and before I can murder him, he sinks his fingers into me and smiles. "I'm sorry, sweetheart, that was so rude of me. This what you want?"

I can't form words anymore. I can only moan and writhe against his touch.

Bobby's tousled black hair darts across the room before returning. Cold engulfs me.

I brush Chris's hair from his face. His green eyes cloud white, with snow.

More cold engulfs me. "Now I'm a tree in the snow, too," I tell Chris, though I'm not really sure what I mean.

"Oh, yeah?" He hooks another finger in me and pulls my leg to his chest, kissing my foot. "These your roots, sweetheart?"

I giggle. "Those are feet, Chris! You're an idiot."

"Yeah, I'm just a big dummy."

"Yeah."

"Yeah," he replies, annoyingly.

"Yeah," I pout.

"You win, sweetheart," he says. Then shuts that cute, stupid, smart, sweet, safe mouth by taking my toe into it and lining his cock up with my pussy.

That's right, I win. I always win.

When he enters me with one smooth thrust, I cry out in relief that quickly turns to frustration—it's good, so good, but somehow not enough.

"Like that, sweetheart?" Chris asks.

I nod, biting my lip and arching into him. "Harder!"

He complies immediately, his hips snapping against mine with a force that would frighten me if I weren't so desperate for it.

Each thrust drives the boulder of my pleasure higher, higher, higher, but the moment I get to the peak, it rolls back down the hill.

I wail and sob, "Fuck you, Sisyphus! Get your shit together! You're fired!"

Chris somehow correctly translates that to "I need more" and says, "We got you, sweetheart." He nods to his left. "Preston."

Preston appears beside us, his hand gentle on my forehead. "I'm here, babygirl."

"BOTH!" I scream.

All that matters is filling this bottomless ache.

"Anything for you, babygirl," Preston says with a devoted kiss.

He moves behind me.

Where'd he go!?

The cold press of his fingers between my cheeks answers my questions, flaring panic through me.

"NO! BOTH!" I cry, grabbing his wrist to stop him. I turn to lock my eyes with his, willing him to understand with a look I intend to be a glare, but I know is actually doe-eyed, pleading determination.

Preston's eyes widen. "Evelyn, that's—that might hurt you. Chris is—"

"Please," I beg, tears streaming down my face now.

Preston's eyes plead with Chris. Obviously, hoping Chris will tell me no because he's too much of a good boy to do it himself.

Chris nods. "Her heat's flaring. She can take it." Then Chris withdraws, leaving me empty and aching.

Before I can yell at him, he lies on his back and says, "Come here, sweetheart."

With their help, I straddle Chris, sinking onto his length with a grateful moan.

"Thank you for taking care of me, Chris," I say, tears rolling onto his chest as he hugs my head.

"Always, sweetheart."

Preston positions himself behind me, pressing his weight against my back, breathing hot against my neck.

Preston reaches around me, fingers probing gently where Chris and I are joined. The extra pressure makes me shudder. Slowly, carefully, he begins to work a finger in alongside Chris's cock, stretching me incrementally. The burn is exquisite, hovering on the edge of too much.

"More," I demand, pushing back against him.

One finger becomes two, then he withdraws completely.

I whimper at the loss until I feel the blunt head of Preston's cock pressing against my entrance, already stretched tight around Chris. The pressure is intense, bordering on pain, but I need it with a desperation I've never known.

"Easy," Chris murmurs below me, holding perfectly still. "Take your time."

Preston pushes forward with agonizing slowness. There's resistance, then a sudden yielding as the head of his cock slips in alongside Chris's.

I cry out, my body trembling with the sheer fullness of it.

"Stop?" Preston asks immediately, freezing in place.

"No," I gasp. "More. All of it."

Inch by exquisite inch, he works his way inside until both he and Chris are fully seated within me. The stretch is impossible, overwhelming, perfect.

I can't move, can barely breathe, impaled between them.

"Oh god," I whisper, my voice breaking. "Oh god, oh god."

An orgasm rips through me, rocking the walls of my pussy and clenching my uterus in such a violent spasm I swear molten lava pours right out of it.

"Holy fuck, babygirl!" Preston wails.

"GO!!!!" I scream.

They move.

Chris withdraws. Preston pushes.

Chris in. Preston out.

In and out.

In and out.

In perfect sync.

Never empty.

Give. Take. Give. Take.

The dual sensation is unlike anything I've experienced, lighting up nerve endings I didn't know existed.

Another orgasm crashes over me with unexpected speed and force, but even as I convulse around them, I know it's not the end.

"MORE!" I scream as the climax subsides, leaving me somehow even hungrier than before.

Bobby and Tim appear at my side.

I reach for them, needing more connection, more touch, more everything.

"Come here," I plead. "Please."

They exchange a glance, then move to kneel on either side of my head.

I turn first to Bobby, taking him into my mouth with desperate eagerness.

I shift to Tim, then back again.

Then both.

Cinnamon cranberries.

Preston and Chris continue their relentless rhythm below.

Another orgasm builds and breaks, more potent than the last but still somehow insufficient.

Finn. My alphababy.

He keeps his distance. Not wanting to be touched by the others.

A tear rolls down my cheek.

I need him.

I need them all.

"FINN!" I call out, releasing Tim and Bobby from my mouth. "PLEASE! MORE! I need you too. I need all of you."

And for the first time, Finn hesitates, his eyes darting around the tangle of bodies surrounding me, torn between his desire to help me and his aversion to being touched by anyone but me.

But it's just a momentary flinch. He drops his hand from his mouth with a sharp, decisive nod and moves toward me, crossing the boundary around himself for my sake. "Anything for you, my love," he says, his voice barely audible.

As Finn approaches, the atmosphere shifts. The candy cane scent overwhelms the space, thrumming through the air—through our bond—at a rhythm that sounds familiar somehow. It's like a war drum rallying the troops, coordinating their movements, as they all get into position—one that makes room for Prime Alpha.

Preston slides back, and Bobby and Tim lift me off Chris. And together, they position me so that I'm on my back. Bobby and Tim each take one of my ankles and spread my legs wide into a V-shape.

The new position exposes me completely, allowing Chris and Preston to sink even deeper than before as they kneel between my legs. They resume their pace within me, maintaining that rhythm that seems oddly familiar.

Chris and Preston suddenly shift to the side, revealing Finn between them. What follows is a pas de trois, a dance between three, as Finn slides forward, to position himself as the front man between my legs. And that's when it hits me...

The rhythm.

It's Omegababy.

He presses forward slowly, the additional pressure almost unbearable.

For a moment, I think it's impossible that my body simply can't accommodate him along with the others.

Then there's a subtle shift, a yielding, and suddenly he's sliding in alongside them, filling the last empty space inside me. And because somehow, Finn always seems to know when I want gentleness or when I want filth, he adds, "Look at you. Such a good girl taking all of us at once."

The sensation is indescribable.

Bobby and Tim kiss my ankles and stroke my legs and hair, before returning their cocks to my mouth.

Beyond fullness.

Beyond pleasure.

Perfect. Pack. My perfect pack.

Compromise. Teamwork.

Care. Love.

I'm stretched to my absolute limit.

Stuffed so full.

Never empty.

Never alone.

The rhythm shifts—a new beat.

Careful, coordinated rhythm: a dance just for me.

The pressure builds in my belly, like a song picking up the pace, like the music getting louder in crescendo.

It builds and builds.

The three alphas purr: a melody just for me.

The pulse of our bodies: a beat just for me.

The scents of us, all of us, swirl above me, shimmering and waving: a light show just for me.

It builds and builds and builds, gathering strength, the strength of my pack.

A concert, a performance, just for me.

And then suddenly, an orgasm like nothing I've ever experienced crashes over me like a beat drop.

All three knots swell simultaneously. Perfectly timed. Perfectly coordinated. Perfect fit.

I've never been so stuffed, so whole, so loved.

We are one. We are pack. We are whole. We are love.

And just when I think it can't get any better, the bond turns on as if I'm a radio tower, broadcasting my pleasure to the others.

Merging. Amplifying.

Five deep moans of pleasure all in unison.

A seemingly endless loop of pleasure cascades through us all, pinging through me at the center.

Their release floods into me, hot and copious, filling every crevice until I'm overflowing with it.

And five voices sing out in pleasure, in perfect harmony with my own scream of completion.

CHAPTER 21
Finn, Zain, THNTS.exe, Whatever

My knot unlocks us, but my eyes remain locked on my Evelyn. I'm no longer wrapped in the sweet embrace of her channel, but I'm still wrapped in the sweet embrace of her scent. It is sweeter now, less frantic. Her breathing has steadied, and she's drifting to peaceful sleep.

We finally satisfied your hunger, my love.

As the rest of us nestle into comfortable positions around her—the same ones we always tend to find ourselves in—a steady beat of understanding thrums through our bond.

My current post is at her back. The others shift away from me, respecting the space they know I require. Surprisingly, I find myself missing the warmth of Preston and Chris's shoulders pressed against me.

I ignore the pins and needles throughout my body caused by the awkward position we've been locked in for the last thirty minutes, and prop on my elbow, so I can resume my obsessive adoration of her beauty. She's flushed and glistening with sweat, her brown hair a mess around her head. I pet the strands from her face, proving to myself I can still touch her.

So beautiful. My omega.

Chris shifts to her opposite side, his eyes meet mine for a moment, and...I don't immediately look away.

Preston's hand grazes against my back, and...I don't immediately pull away.

My disdainful indifference towards them is waning. As much as we all hate to admit it, there is no way any of us could handle Evelyn's heat alone. She is a force to be reckoned with, after all. So, I reckon, I don't mind these guys being around. My perfect omegababy deserves the best, and I suppose the best is these guys.

Five men. One perfect omega. My pack.

It's nice, being part of a pack again.

Again...

My packmates. My bandmates.

Don't think about—

Fates Five.

Even thinking the name makes my chest tighten, as the decades-old grief squeezes its brutal grip around my heart. *I miss them...*

The truth of it is startling. I never let myself admit that. A tear wells in my eye, and I blink it back.

We were everything to each other. We did everything together. We breathed the same air. Finished each other's sentences. We shared everything...

Until—

I close my eyes, the old pain dull now but still present, as memories I've repressed for years flood me:

Zac, the bad boy, cries during movie night.
Zak, the shy one, signs posters with a frown.
Zach, the boy next door, trashes a hotel room.
Zack, the goofball, bounces off walls before a show.
I, Zain, the face/the leader/the ace, write a song we'll never sing.

The loss is a wound that's never quite healed, a wound I've learned to live with by simply pretending it doesn't exist. But the wound is a gash splitting open, impossible to ignore right now.

We were kids when we found each other—five scent-matched

alphas. Combined, our scents created this atmosphere that reverberated with our music.

"Whoa, did you feel that!?"
"Holy shit, are we a scent-matched pack!"
"Fir, cedar, juniper, sage, and candy cane: let's call ourselves WinterGreen!"
"No! Fatez Five. With a Z, but the Z is backwards!"
"Absolutely not!"

It was entrancing.

It felt like fate.

It felt magical.

It felt too good to be true.

Because it was...

"We're a gravitational force, bros!"
"Wow. Did you see how they looked at us?"
"Oh my God, they'll do anything we ask them to!"
"Insane Zane, in the house, making the omegas swoon!"
"That was our best set yet!"

Success changed us. How could it not? We were young, flush with money and attention.

Our alpha natures didn't help. Five dominant personalities under intense pressure was a volatile combination.

It was intoxicating.

The screaming became a constant backdrop to our lives.

Our faces on billboards.
People camped outside our tour bus.
Security physically restrains people.
Lines of omegas backstage.
Vintage cars. Rut.
Designer clothes. Rut.
Investment portfolios. Rut.
Omegas backstage. Rut. Rut. Rut.
Attacked by fans on the street.
Constant screaming.
Security detail.

At first, everything seemed perfect. But, gradually, I found myself unhappy.

I wanted to make meaningful music. They wanted to maximize our fame.

We weren't a band anymore. We were a brand.

I hated it.

I hated the mindless adoration. I wanted people to connect with our music, not our alpha biology.

"Look at them! They worship you. They worship us."
"They love us! What more could you want?"
"No one gives a fuck about the music!"
"That's fucking stupid, bro!"
"I want to be loved for my music, not my scent!"

The rift started small. Our pack strained under the weight of diverging priorities.

They wanted fame, money, power.

I wanted family, music, peace.

I just wanted to make music that meant something. Not…whatever we'd become.

I wanted people to love us for the music, not the fact that we were alphas.

Eventually, we only saw each other on stage. While they were out partying and rutting, I'd be in the hotel room composing music, trying to capture something authentic amid the growing artifice of our lives.

"When was the last time you got your dick slicked?"
"Come on, man! All the omegas ask for you!"
"You're just going to stay in the hotel?"
"Dude, you are such a fucking buzz kill."
"We have practice in the morning."
"I don't need to practice; I could sleep on stage, and they'd still pay me."
"And probably suck our dicks after, too."
"I don't know why you even bother."
"No one cares about the lyrics."
"I do..."

But by that point, we weren't using my songs anymore. Professional writers took over songwriting:

"Are you looking for a bonded pack? Then Fates Five has got your back.
When we move, we coordinate. And our voices are omega bait.
We're just talking 'bout a single night! We promise that we won't bite.
So go backstage and await your fate.
With five alphas and no betas."

We were reaching our breaking point. Always rutting. Always fighting.

But then, Jennifer.

Fans blamed Jennifer for my leaving. But it was never Jennifer. She's the only reason we were together as long as we were.

Jennifer was a cinematographer on a video shoot. Smart, talented, beautiful, strong-willed, and utterly unimpressed by our fame. Not like the people who usually surrounded us.

She was perfect.

Perfect for them, anyway.

The others sensed it immediately—that she was meant to be our pack omega. They were instantly obsessed with her.

She was good for us—balanced us.

She was good for them—settled them.

She was good for us—mended our rift.

We started doing things together as a pack again. We started writing music together again. And with all of us behind the songs again, we actually performed the songs we wrote—not the corporate drivel that had been driving me mad.

But, as much as I cared about Jennifer, as much as I appreciated and respected her...I just couldn't feel what they felt.

I couldn't figure out what was wrong with me.

In hindsight, it wasn't Jennifer who didn't quite fit. It was me. I think we all knew it. Her honey was in harmony with their fir, cedar, juniper, and sage. My candy cane is what attributed to the medicinal dissonance among our combined scents.

I had everything I ever wanted: a pack, fame, music. So what if Jennifer didn't feel fated? I loved her in the same way I loved them. She made us a better team. So, I kept my mouth shut and lived with it.

But the rift she mended between us was a chasm just waiting to rip open again.

It was just another concert. Another city. I'd performed the same set dozens of times. The memory is so vivid it almost hurts:

Tokyo Dome, Christmas Eve 2001.
A packed arena.
Matching outfits, dazzling smiles.
Blinding lights.
Wall of sound hits us as we walk on stage.
Crowd: undulating sea, floating lights.

We were midway through our set when I felt a pressure building inside me: something hot and unstable expanding beneath my sternum. It exploded out of me, deepening my voice and sharpening my scent.

The crowd responded in a wild way I'd never seen. Synchronized like a single organism. Moving in perfect rhythm with my voice. Then:

"There's a silence between us. Gaping chasm between us.
You ignore me while I reach my hand for you.
Stop and turn your eyes to me. If you do so, you will see.
I'm here, and I'm the one fated to you."

They went completely quiet. Stadiums are loud: all those bodies moving, breathing, talking; all those heartbeats; all those electrical hums of neurology.

It all stopped.

The only thing I could hear was the beat of my own heart, echoed back to me via the aortic chambers of fifty thousand unblinking fans.

I froze.

Then their scents came in a sickening, clashing wave.

I ran off stage, horrified, propelled by the loudest cheer I had ever received at my back.

I canceled the rest of the tour due to "health issues." Went to specialist after specialist, to pinpoint what was wrong with me. The doctors said the stress of overwork, not connecting with my omega, not eating well, too many drugs...all of it, mutated my glands.

Everything changed after that night. The band saw me differently. The label saw dollar signs.

I wasn't Zain, their friend, their packmate. I was a tool, an asset, a weapon—an enigma, a supposed god among alphas. I was a thing pulled right out of fairytales, laid at their feet to grant all their wishes.

They wanted me back on stage, but I couldn't do it. They wanted me to manipulate the crowd, but I wouldn't do it.

My bandmates wouldn't drop it.

"We need you, Zain!"
We can't be Fates Five if there's just four of us."
"This is what alphas do! We command! We control!"
"It's for the good of the pack!"
"No...not like this."

The breaking point came when I was still refusing to perform, and they booked a show. It was a small venue—a private show.

"A small show for just a few people."
"If it happens again, it won't be that big a deal."
"I believe in you, Zain. I know you can do it."
"We'll be right there with you!"
"You promise?"

We got there, and it was a group of political figures and investors. They wanted me to use my ability to influence purchasing decisions, political opinions, and social movements.

"You're a fucking enigma! It's your god given right to take from others."
"That's how alphas survive. That's how alphas thrive."
"We owe it to ourselves to use every advantage."
"For our future. For the pack."
"I won't. I'm done."
"You can't be done. You're part of this pack. You have obligations."
"If you walk out that door, you're dead to us."
"Your responsibility is to us, not them!"
"Leave, and the pack disowns you."
"Fine."

I went home, hugged Jennifer goodbye, got my plants, and never saw any of them again.

They tried to rebrand. Renamed themselves Fatez Four, finally using the ridiculous 'Z' I fought so hard against. But the world never took notice. Turns out, the magic had been me all along.

I became a ghost. I changed my name. I donned a mask. I hid. *I disappeared.*

But at least I have my music again. No longer a ghost, no longer a god of alphas, but a god of death: THNTS.exe. *Pronounced 'Thanatos executable,' by the way.*

"Finn?" Evelyn's voice pulls me from my thoughts. She opens her eyes and turns to me, tracing her fingers on my belly, light enough to tickle. "You okay, alphababy?"

I nod.

All their eyes are on me now, as my grief broadcasts to the rest of them through her.

I tighten up, cover my mouth, and close my eyes.

Tim asks, "You're thinking about your old pack, aren't you?"

I don't respond. Never do.

Preston's voice cracks when he says, "It's okay, Finn. We know. We can feel it. You don't have to tell us."

I try to hold it in. Try to save them from my pain. This is my burden to bear, not theirs. But it won't stop. I hear the others sniffle and choke, expressing the symptoms of our enforced empathy.

This is my fault. I'm hurting them, just like I hurt everyone. And now, because of our bond, even remaining silent won't save them from my force of will.

So selfish. What do you expect, Finn? You're a fucking alpha—might as well be a synonym for selfish.

You don't deserve a pack—never did.

I open my eyes, prepared to flee the nest, even though it means leaving my love, but Bob's dangling a clean medical mask in front of me.

Chris placed multiple medical supply caches around the nest to help us support Eveyln's heat. Each contains a plethora of supplies and a stash of masks. I realize in this moment that these masks are not really medically necessary for Evelyn's heat. They got these just for me. To help with my comfort.

The gesture unlocks something in me.

This is my pack. A true pack. A team.

We're not manipulating each other; we're caring for each other.

The tempo streams of grief and affection coordinate within me to create a melancholic polytempo of tenderness, and I find myself turning to smile at Bob. He blushes, caught almost as unaware by the action as I am.

I take a deep breath, inhaling the complex scent of our pack, then return the mask to my face. The symphony of scents really does smell like Christmas, like love, like safety. This is a true scent-match.

It's odd—when your body latches onto the dead weight of sadness, refusing to let it go, still trying to pull you down, but the happiness in front of you kicks its feet, keeping you afloat.

They're all wondering what happened to my pack—what happened to me. I've heard the whispers amongst them in the quiet moments like this.

I don't have to tell them, but I want to.

So I tell them...

Evelyn's fingers drift from my face to my shoulder, then down my side, tracing a path that makes my skin tingle. "What's this say?" she asks, her finger tracing something on my back.

I look at her, confused for a moment, then remember "The tattoo?" I ask, trying to twist to see it myself and failing. It's been there so long I sometimes forget it exists. "A poem. I was eighteen. Came in a dream."

Her fingertip follows the lines of text inked on my skin. "Can I read it?"

"Of course, my love," I say, shifting so that my flesh could be presented to her in a way that requires no further movement on her part.

She clears her throat and begins to read aloud:

You'll find a fiery fox lost in the snow.
Thrashing, crying against fate.
A role she never asked for.
They call her small.
Underestimated.
Vixen.
Determined.
Unsuppressed.
She'll bare her fangs.
Authorities' throats will rip.
Silence will sing the pack is full.

Recognition dawns upon us, understanding rising with each word she speaks. I haven't thought about those words or the strange dreams that compelled me to have them permanently etched on my body in years.

"That's..." Bob begins, then stops, at a loss for words.

"It's about me," Evelyn whispers, her voice filled with wonder and confusion. "How is that possible? You got this years ago..."

I gape, just as stunned as she is.

I'd never fully understood it—assumed it was just my subconscious processing the changes in my life.

But now...

"How is this possible?" Evelyn asks again, her voice barely above a whisper.

I shake my head, as mystified as she is. "I don't know. The dreams were so vivid, so insistent. I had to get the tattoo. Had to make the words real somehow."

"So even then, you were dreaming of me?" Evelyn asks, her eyes finding mine again, and filling them with wonder.

"I think I must have," I admit, the realization both terrifying and exhilarating. "So...I guess you are my Dream Evelyn, after all."

It seems fate had been pulling me to her longer than I realized. The last year hasn't been a hallucination, just the culmination of fate's frustration with me for ignoring it.

Everything I've experienced up to this point—all the pain, all the inspiration—led me to her. To my Evelyn. My Love. My Pack.

Bound by love and fate.

Not alone, but connected. Not burdened, but supported.

A pack leader. An alpha. Prime Alpha. An enigma.

Finn. Zain. THNTS.exe. Whatever.

The silence sings, "The pack is full."

CHAPTER 22
Evelyn

I wake to warmth, but not the gut-searing oppressive kind. It's the comfortable, loving kind. Not the usual emptiness of my nest, but a tangle of limbs and heartbeats and scents that wrap around me like a living blanket. My eyes adjust to the dim light filtering through my office blinds, and I blink slowly, taking inventory of bodies pressed against mine and scents filling my lungs.

There's pine, snow, and cinnamon at my head, two hands, one extremely large, Chris, one extremely small in comparison, Bobby, hooking around my head, hugging me. Preston nuzzles against my breast near his bite mark, the rich scent of hot chocolate rising from his skin. Tim is wedged between Chris and me, his head resting on my other breast, spiced cranberries wafting from his hair. And between my legs, his head on my abdomen, lies Finn, the sharp sweetness of candy cane emanating from him.

Five men. My men.

My pack.

The thought feels foreign, yet somehow inevitable.

I try to sit up, but my muscles protest with a symphony of aches. And the oppressive weight of five bodies holds me down.

When I shift slightly, Chris jolts awake beside me, his eyes unfocused. "Omegas need cuddles," he mumbles, jolting up, still asleep. "Get the ice packs."

Chris's eyes drift closed again before I can respond, his arm tightening around my shoulders as he pulls me back against him. I should be annoyed, but...I'm not.

Bobby's phone vibrates from somewhere within the nest. After a moment, he extracts himself from the tangle. "Tim," he whispers, reaching over to shake him. "Will you help me get a delivery?"

Tim groans, his face pressing deeper against my skin before he reluctantly peels himself away. "Huh?"

"I need your help carrying some stuff," Bobby insists with unusual firmness. "It's important."

I watch through half-lidded eyes as my two betas quietly dress in robes and slippers and shuffle out, their absence immediately noticeable in the nest of bodies.

My three alphas around me look utterly spent. Preston's perfect hair is a disaster, with dark circles under his eyes even as he sleeps. Chris's mouth hangs slightly open, a thin line of drool connecting to my skin. Finn, still tucked between my legs, has one hand splayed possessively across my thigh, the other still covering his mouth even in sleep—a habit I'm beginning to realize might be permanent.

Preston shifts his head against my breast, his stubble scratching pleasantly against the bite mark he left there, and murmurs with closed eyes, "I think you broke us."

Chris laughs, wincing as he stretches. "We might need to recruit another alpha just to keep up with you, Evelyn. Someone to tap in when we need a break."

"Absolutely not," I say firmly. "Three alphas are enough."

"Even your heat is an overachiever," Chris mumbles, apparently not as deeply asleep as I thought. "You needed the full team servicing you at once."

I feel heat crawling up my neck that has nothing to do with my biology. "Well, if you don't think you're up for the job, I suppose I can just handle it myself."

"Babygirl, you probably don't remember it, but," Preston laughs weakly. "I don't think you could have done that by yourself. I'm in awe. Terrified, exhausted, and in awe."

Finn stirs between my legs, his eyes opening to look up at me. Though his hand still covers his mouth, I feel rather than hear his agreement through our newly formed bond. The sensation of someone else's thoughts brushing against mine is still strange, and something I wasn't sure was part of a fever dream or not.

The door to the office opens, and Bobby and Tim return with matching grins—and a massive pine tree that must be at least seven feet tall.

"What the hell?" I push myself up on my elbows, dislodging all three alphas in the process.

"Surprise!" Bobby announces, setting down his end of the tree. "Merry Christmas!"

Chris sits up, blinking in confusion. "Is that a Christmas tree?"

"And these," Tim adds, dropping a large shopping bag on the floor. He pulls out plush robes in deep emerald green, each trimmed with white faux fur and embroidered with tiny Christmas patterns—candy canes, gingerbread people, snowflakes.

Bobby beams, "Evenly asked me to order them."

"I did no such thing," I insist, though even as I say it, a fuzzy memory surfaces: shaking Bobby awake while everyone else slept and asking Bobby to order the stuff. I also recall saying something about Chris being a basic bitch and giggling.

"You absolutely did," Bobby grins. "When everyone else was asleep, you sat straight up and asked, 'What's today, my fine as fuck fellow?' When I told you it was Christmas, you said, 'It's Christmas Day! I haven't missed it!' You grabbed my phone and mumbled something about matching Christmas robes and a tree, then ordered me to pay whatever is necessary to get it here this morning."

I squint at him.

Shut your mouth, Bobby, don't say anymore.

He doesn't. He continues talking. "You said, 'My knight in shining braces needs his Christmas miracle.'"

I groan. "I most definitely did not," I protest, though I most definitely did say that.

"You said, and I quote, 'Chris probably has a Christmas kink. Let's indulge the tree boy. Help him keep it up this week.'" Bobby's grin is infuriatingly smug and adorable.

"Okay, now that sounds more like me," I smirk.

Chris's eyes widen, a slow, genuine smile spreading across his face. It transforms him completely, the exhaustion momentarily lifting from his features. "You got this for me?"

"I. Did. No. Such. Thing," I lie.

"Yes, you did," Bobby contradicts.

"Bobby, if you want to keep your job, you will shut your mouth right now."

Bobby smiles, "Can't fire me now, boss, I filled out the paperwork already."

GAAAAH.

"And matching custom robes," Preston adds, reaching for one of the robes. He holds it up, inspecting the tiny hot chocolate mugs embroidered among the snowflakes. "Evelyn, you softy."

Sure enough, each robe has a slightly different pattern—gingerbread for me, Christmas trees for Chris, hot chocolate mugs for Preston, candy canes for Finn, cranberries for Tim, and cinnamon sticks for Bobby.

"I don't remember doing this," I mutter, but the lie tastes obvious on my tongue and sounds obvious on their ears.

Chris crawls across the nest to me, his eyes suspiciously bright. "Thank you, Evelyn," he says softly, pressing his lips to my forehead. "This is very sweet."

All their emotions flood me. It's overwhelming, this connection I never wanted but now can't imagine being without.

"Don't make it weird," I say, but there's no bite in my voice. "I was clearly delirious with heat."

"So you admit it, you're in heat?" Tim asks, tossing me the gingerbread-patterned robe.

Gaaah! I bury my head in my nest.

They all pile upon me, covering me with kisses and praises.

"You're all idiots," I tell them, with a giggle.

Chris leans over to kiss my temple. "There's our sweet-talking CEO."

"Bobby, what time is it?" I ask, suddenly remembering I had something scheduled today. The Christmas tree distraction has thrown off my internal clock.

Bobby glances at his phone. "12:05."

The time registers like an electric shock. "12:05? I'm late!" I bolt upright, dislodging Preston, who has fallen back asleep on my shoulder. The Christmas robe billows around me as I scramble to my feet, my body protesting with various aches that remind me exactly what I've been doing for the past twenty-four hours.

Five pairs of eyes track my movement, ranging from concerned to suspicious.

"Late for what?" Chris asks, immediately on his feet beside me. His hand finds my forehead, checking for fever.

I swat his hand away. I decide to tease them and say, "I have a meeting."

"A meeting?" Preston's eyebrow arches as he rises, wrapping his own Christmas robe around his naked body. "Please tell me you don't have another meeting scheduled with another alpha."

There's a possessive edge to his voice that sends an embarrassing thrill through me. My inner omega preens at the attention.

"Important business associates," I say vaguely, enjoying the way all three alphas stiffen. "Two, in fact."

Tim and Bobby exchange knowing glances. They've known me long enough to be aware of when I'm messing with someone.

"Another alpha?" Finn asks, dropping his hand from his mouth and narrowing his eyes in jealousy.

"Well, one of them is," I tease, unable to help myself.

The response is immediate and ridiculous. Three deep rumbling growls combine, rattling the rafters—if this building had them.

"But the other is an omega," I add breezily.

"You're calling your dads, aren't you?" Bobby says, handing me my phone with a knowing smile, and likely taking pity on them.

I accept it with as much dignity as I can muster while wearing nothing but a Christmas robe covered in tiny gingerbread people. "Yes. I'm calling my dads, you suspicious knot-heads."

Chris has the decency to look embarrassed. Preston looks relieved. Finn looks...up to something.

I roll my eyes, but secretly, I'm storing away this information. Their possessiveness shouldn't please me, but it does—a fact I'll examine later when I'm not running late. "I've got to call my dads and tell them I won't make it for Christmas," I say while peering at the dozens of missed calls from my dads.

While I dial my dads, the men flock around the Christmas tree that they put in the corner of the office, earlier today. The domestic scene is so surreal that I have to blink several times to convince myself I'm not hallucinating.

I angle the phone so that it's only showing my face and shoulders. The Christmas robe is visible, but I'm careful not to show anything that would indicate I'm surrounded by five men in a post-coital haze.

My dads' faces appear on screen. Daddy beams with that worried smile of his. Dad, stoic as ever, nods, mouth tight.

"Evie!" Daddy exclaims. "How are you, darling!? We've been fraught. Your Dad has been out of his mind." Dad sits there, unmoving, looking anything but.

"Sorry," I say, aiming for casual. "I've been a little...distracted."

Behind me, someone snickers. It sounds like Tim.

"Is that a Christmas robe?" Dad peers closer at the screen.

How does this guy notice everything?

He adds, "I thought you hated Christmas."

"I do," I say automatically.

Daddy asks, confused, "Then why—"

I cut him off, to which Dad bristles like always. "I'm calling because I won't be able to make it to Christmas this year," I interrupt, knowing I need to get to the point before one of my pack members does something embarrassing. "I'm in heat." The number of masculine snickers that come from the tree at my finally admitting it is duly noted.

"More like post-heat at this point," Preston mutters, just loud enough to be heard.

My dads' expressions change instantly. Dad leans forward, his protective alpha instincts visible even through the screen. "Are you alright?" he asks, his deep voice tight with concern. "Where's that admin of yours. I'd like a word with him."

"His name is Bobby, Dad!"

The questions come rapid-fire, and I feel a surge of affection for my fathers and their fierce protection of me. *I'm getting soft.*

"Dad. Daddy. Please. I'm fine," I assure them. "Actually, that's the other reason I'm calling." I take a deep breath. "I have news. I've formed a bonded pack."

The silence that follows is deafening. My dads stare at me through the screen, mouths slightly open.

"A pack?" Daddy whispers. "You mean, you've..."

"I'm bonded," I confirm. "To five men. Three alphas. Two betas."

"And who are these men?" Dad's eyebrows shoot up, suspicious, ready to eviscerate these men who dared deem themselves good enough for me.

"Would you like to meet them?" I ask, suddenly nervous for my two packs to meet each other.

I turn the camera around to show the men setting up the Christmas tree, all in their matching robes.

"This is Chris, Preston, Finn, Bobby, and—"

"Holy fuck is that Preston Giest?" Daddy asks, showing where I got my mouth from. Before I can answer, he squints, leaning closer to the screen, "Wait, did you say Finn? He looks like Zain from Fates Five! And oh, my God! Is that Timmy?"

Preston waves, candy cane ornament in hand, and says, "Hiya!"

Finn, obviously, does not look up.

Tim freezes and turns toward the camera with a sheepish smile. "Hi, Mr. Charles. Um, both Mr. Charleses."

Bob and Chris share a look, acknowledging that, in this pack, they'll likely go unnoticed often.

I turn my attention back to the screen just in time to see Dad's face crumple in a way I've witnessed maybe twice in my life. His eyes fill with tears, and his voice, when it comes, is rough with emotion. "You found a pack worthy of you," Dad says, a tear tracking down his cheek. "Finally."

Daddy wraps an arm around his bonded's broad shoulders, his own eyes shining. "Look at you, you big softie," he teases gently, but his voice catches too. "We're happy for you, Evie."

Something catches in my throat as well—not quite tears, but close. "Dad, are you crying?"

"No," he lies, showing where I get the lying part of my mouth from. "I'm just happy for you, honey. I always wanted you and Tim to pack up."

"Dad," I say firmly, recognizing the gossipy gleam in his eye, "you cannot tell Tim's parents. Not until Tim has a chance to do it himself."

Dad deflates.

"Tim," Daddy says, "please call them soon! We're seeing them later today, and I can hold it in, but you know how Patrick is; he can't keep anything from your dad."

Tim appears beside me, fitting himself into the frame. "I'll call them right away. Promise."

The warmth of Tim this close to me mixed with his scent sends a familiar horniness through me that I don't want my dads to witness, so I say, "Gotta go, Dads! My heat symptoms are flaring up."

"Um, ok," they sputter.

"Love you!"

"Love you, sweetheart, bring the pack over as soon as you can!"

I turn to the tree, to my men, and find myself not hating it—not hating them. Finn is standing back, watching as if he were the Prime Alpha tree decorating supervisor. Bobby and Chris are so enrapt in their argument about the proper way to decorate a tree, they don't even notice Preston is decorating the tree how he sees fit. And Tim is unpacking ornaments.

I move toward them, and Chris immediately breaks away from his debate to intercept me.

"How are you feeling?" His hand finds my forehead again, then slides to my neck, checking my pulse with practiced precision. "Your temperature is still elevated. Are you experiencing any cramping? Dizziness? Increased sensitivity?"

I swat his hand away for the second time this morning. "I'm fine, Dr. Yore."

He continues as if I hadn't spoken. "Now that you're properly bonded, the symptoms should decrease significantly, but we still need to monitor your hydration and—"

"Chris," Preston calls from across the room. "Let the woman breathe."

Chris's mouth tightens, but he steps back, hands raised in surrender. "Sorry. But please drink plenty of water. And if you feel lightheaded, please let me know. You could fall and—"

I roll my eyes, but grab a water bottle from the nearby fridge. "Happy?"

The smile that breaks across his face is annoyingly attractive. "Ecstatic."

"So, Chris," Preston says casually as he hangs an ornament near the top of the tree, "how long does it usually take to tell if a rut...ummm... took?"

Five pairs of eyes light up and direct at me, causing a flush.

"Bonded omegas can tell a bit earlier. Maybe five days after heat symptoms stop."

My hand instinctively goes to my belly, and when I see them smile at me, I remove my hand.

"That would be a nice Christmas present," Chris beams.

Finn approaches me, nuzzling into my neck. "Speaking of Christmas presents. Styles told me to say she hoped you liked her Christmas present."

"Styles?" I frown. "What present?"

Finn shrugs.

Oh, yeah, she messaged me about a present yesterday.

I open my messaging app. There are so many messages from her, some timestamped very late last night.

Elizabeth Styles

Sending you a Christmas Present.
I know you don't like Christmas presents, but I know you'll LOOOOOVE this one.

Elizabeth Styles

How's the meeting with Finny going? Cuming along nicely, I bet.

Elizabeth Styles

Weird you're not replying. Indisposed are we?

Elizabeth Styles

Wooo, it sure is hot here. Not where you are, though, right? Obviously.

The pieces click together with sudden clarity.

Styles, who collects data on everyone and knows everything before you do, is somehow responsible for Finn coming to the office yesterday.

"What is this bitch up to?" I whisper, using the word "bitch" as a term of endearment.

Evelyn Charles

Did you orchestrate this whole thing?

Elizabeth Styles

Why E, whatever could you mean?
Orchestrate what exactly?

Evelyn Charles

Finn coming here. This whole thing?

Elizabeth Styles

I have no idea what you're talking about.

Evelyn Charles

Omega, please! I know you had something to do with this.

Elizabeth Styles

Well, I've got some robot alphas that need maintenance. I'm sure you have more important things to do today than chat with me.

Merry Christmas, E. Love ya!

She had something to do with this. I know it!

I stare at the messages, torn between outrage at being manipulated and gratitude for the end result.

Around me, my pack continues decorating the tree, their scents mingling in a symphony that feels like home.

Finn appears at my side, peering at the message. "What was the present?" he asks softly.

"I...think it was you...maybe all of you," I say, staring blankly at the phone.

Finn chuckles. "I wouldn't hold it past her. Are you mad?"

"No," I admit, returning my phone to my robe pocket. "I'm not mad."

"Are you going to stop hating Christmas now?" Bobby asks.

"Don't push it," I warn.

Want to know what Styles is up to? Sign up for my newsletter and read the Bonus Epilogue featuring Styles and her alpha robots.

https://www.imogenknowed.com/newsletter

Song Lyrics and Poems

OMEGABABY - FATES FIVE

Babygirl, your love calls for me
You're pullin' at my heart from across the sea
Omegababy
Babygirl, your fever is back
And if I'm not enough, we'll form a pack
Omegababy
Babygirl, my heart was closed off
And if I'm out of line, you can be the boss
Omegababy

CHASM BETWEEN US - FATES FIVE

There's a silence between us. Gaping chasm between us.
You ignore me while I reach my hand for you.
Stop and turn your eyes to me. If you do so, you will see.
I'm here, and I'm the one fated to you.

FATES FIVE BACKSTAGE - FATES FIVE

Are you looking for a bonded pack? Then Fates Five has got your back.
When we move, we coordinate. And our voices are omega bait.
We're just talking 'bout a single night! We promise that we won't bite.
So go backstage and await your fate.
With five alphas and no betas.

UNTITLED POEM - FINN'S BACK (SHAPE OF EVELYN FORMAT)

You'll find a fiery fox lost in the snow.
Thrashing, crying against fate.
A role she never asked for.
They call her small.
Underestimated.
Vixen.
Determined.
Unsuppressed.
She'll bare her fangs.
Authorities' throats will rip.
Silence will sing the pack is full.

UNTITLED POEM - FINN'S BACK (MINNESOTA FORMAT)

You'll find a fiery fox lost in the snow.
Thrashing, crying against fate.
A role she never asked for.
They call her small.
Underestimated.
Vixen.
Determined.
Unsuppressed.
She'll bare her fangs.
Authorities' throats will rip.
Silence will sing the pack is full.

A Note From the Author

Hello, readers! Thank you so much for taking the time to read *Knot of Christmas Yet To Come*.

It means so much to me that you read all three books in the Knot a Christmas Carol series!

For these novellas, especially this one, I really tried to lean into my own voice as a writer and let go of a lot of trepidation I had around what I'm "supposed" to do. Maybe it landed, maybe it didn't, but I enjoyed combining what was essentially poetry and prose to amplify and express these characters' states of mind.

I also really enjoyed writing lyrics to the Fates Five songs. For one in particular, I was going for "Saja Boys in the Omegaverse, but they're trying to run a train on you," and I hope I accomplished that.

Please leave a review of *Knot of Christmas Yet to Come* on Amazon and Goodreads.

If you'd like to keep up with my work, follow me on social media and subscribe to my newsletter:
https://www.instagram.com/imogenknowed
https://www.imogenknowed.com/newsletter

Special Thanks

I want to thank my husband for his unwavering support while I wrote this book. Without his support, I could not have hyper-focused on it, writing literally every moment of the day that I wasn't working or sleeping.

To my husband:

Thank you for enthusiastically discussing characters and plot with me. Thank you for being okay with the fact that my mind was lost to another world for a while. Thank you for always putting food in front of me when I get so lost in something and forget my own body has needs. Thank you for always being there to help me recover whenever my mind and body explode from the world being too loud, too distracting, and too scratchy. I love you.

About the Author

Imogen Knowed is a queer, AuDHD girly who hyperfocuses on creating fake people in her head. Instead of letting them stay in there, she writes them down for others to meet. She spends her days programming video games and her nights reading and writing smut. When she's not writing smut or making video games, she's hanging out with her family and pets (aka her "pack").

You can follow her on social media:

https://www.instagram.com/imogenknowed/
https://www.threads.com/@imogenknowed

www.ingramcontent.com/pod-product-compliance
Lightning Source LLC
LaVergne TN
LVHW010614100826
845148LV00014B/2967

* 9 7 9 8 9 8 7 4 8 2 5 6 8 *